SHERLOCK HOLMES

The King's Diamond

Christopher D. Abbott

Copyright © 2023 Christopher D. Abbott

Edited by Scott Pearson
SCOTT-PEARSON.COM

All rights reserved.
ISBN: 9798373196093 – ISBN: 9798372864207 (pbk.)

CDANABBOTT.COM

First Edition

With special thanks to Scott Pearson, Aaron Rosenberg, Richard Sutton, and Rob Reddan.

This is a work of fiction. Names, characters, places, and incidents are products of the author's imagination or are used fictitiously and are not to be construed as real. Any resemblance to actual events, locales, organisations, or persons, living or dead, is entirely coincidental.

Other Titles

MYSTERY: THE DIES SERIES
Sir Laurence Dies
Dr. Chandrix Dies

MYSTERY: THE WATSON CHRONICLES
SHERLOCK HOLMES: *A Scandalous Affair*
SHERLOCK HOLMES: *The Curse of Pharaoh*
SHERLOCK HOLMES: *The Langsdale House Mystery*
SHERLOCK HOLMES: *The Black Lantern*
SHERLOCK HOLMES: *Broken Glass*
SHERLOCK HOLMES: *Mystery at Granholm Asylum*
SHERLOCK HOLMES: *The Second Door*
SHERLOCK HOLMES: *Midnight Fire*
SHERLOCK HOLMES: *Cases by Candlelight*
SHERLOCK HOLMES: *The Tiger's Claws*
SHERLOCK HOLMES: *The King's Diamond*
SHERLOCK HOLMES: *An Unlucky Thief*

FANTASY: THE SONGS OF THE OSIRIAN SERIES
Songs of the Osirian [Book 1]
Rise of the Jackal King [Book 2]
Daughter of Ra [Book 3]
Citadel of Ra [Book 4]
Songs of the Osirian: Companion

SUPERNATURAL/HORROR
Progenitor

CONTENTS

Other Titles

Introduction	2
Chapter One	4
Chapter Two	15
Chapter Three	26
Chapter Four	41
Chapter Five	53
Chapter Six	67
Chapter Seven	77
Chapter Eight	86
Chapter Nine	96
Chapter Ten	105
Epilogue	123
About the Author	128

SHERLOCK HOLMES

The King's Diamond

Introduction

I'd spent several days unpacking my office and organising old manuscripts and other trinkets I'd gained through my long association with Sherlock Holmes, after my oldest son had assisted me in decorating it. There were boxes of case notes open, and I hardly knew where to start. When I came across a small red box that brought back such an avalanche of memories, I quickly unclasped it and smiled at the British Empire Medal within. As clean as the day Queen Victoria had pinned it to my chest. I admit seeing it again caused a somewhat meretricious effect upon me. I sat down and recalled the detail of the case, *The King's Diamond*, whose conclusion had prompted Queen Victoria to award it.

Retirement leaves one with many hours in the day to fill, and lately I've taken on the mantle of the curator of my private Sherlock Holmes library. I thumbed through the cases and found several I knew I wanted to get published. There was the case of *Her Missing Red Pin*, where Holmes and I assisted a young woman to recover one of her father's odd collection of jewelled pins he'd left to her. But the case notes I wanted to find were not here. Eventually, I remembered it was locked in my old tin-box secured safety at the bank.

There are some of our cases that Holmes decreed the

world was not yet ready to read – this being one. As plenty of time has passed and those events were no longer scandalous nor sensational, I decided the case could now be presented to my public. I stopped what I was doing and made the journey into town, collecting the manuscript from the bank. My wife checked through it and I left her to decide if I should make the date explicit. She recommended I leave it as I originally wrote it. So, after a few adjustments here and there, I sent it off to my publisher.

The King's Diamond started easily enough. Sherlock Holmes and I had just finished our breakfast and were smoking a morning pipe when Mrs Hudson ushered Queen Victoria's private secretary, Colonel Alexander Crowhurst, into our rooms. So, dear reader, once again, the game is afoot!

John H. Watson, MD (Retd)
11th December 1925

Chapter One

'Her Majesty's case has been woefully mishandled from the onset.'

It was on a cold mid-spring Tuesday morning that Mr Sherlock Holmes and I would find ourselves sat opposite a very special messenger in our rooms of 221b Baker Street, that being Colonel Alexander Crowhurst, who introduced himself as a member of Queen Victoria's private staff. The regal-looking gentleman of around sixty – his red hair greying at the tips – sat patiently as Mrs Hudson finished pouring the tea, giving her a polite nod when she finished and withdrew to leave us to our discussions.

Colonel Crowhurst took a long sip of the potent brew before setting his cup down and turning his troubled brow to my friend.

'I appreciate your seeing me at such short notice, Mr Holmes,' the old soldier said.

Sherlock Holmes, who remained standing by the mantle, set his cup into its saucer and carefully placed it onto a side-table. His long arm then retrieved the cherry-wood pipe from the rack – a preferred choice when listening to the narrative of a client – which he filled with tobacco from the Persian slipper and soon lit. Holmes eventually blew a cloud of smoke into the room and took his chair opposite our distinguished guest. He scrutinised every inch of the man before finally pulling the pipe from his mouth and pointing it at him.

'Let's dispense with any further pleasantries, Colonel,' said Holmes. 'Instead, you might spend the time explaining the rather grotesque incompetence that has led you to consult with me on a subject that, I deduce, ought to have come around a week past?'

Sometimes Holmes's moods could make him entirely intolerable, and this was one of them. Most men who were subjected to his rather enigmatic and often unemotional scrutiny – especially those disapproving and critically coarse observations – might take offense to such brusqueness, but to Colonel Crowhurst's credit he not only seemed unaffected by it, but actually appeared to agree with my friend's judgement.

'Your assessment of the situation is quite correct, Mr Holmes,' the colonel voiced. 'But how?'

'Several things. Your beard for one,' said Holmes, as if that was explanation enough. 'A week's growth, I should estimate.'

'Slightly longer,' Crowhurst replied with a deep sigh. 'But I cannot see—'

'There is no mystery to it, Colonel,' my friend said. 'When a man's lifelong habit of daily shaving is suddenly upended, it suggests a calamitous situation has occurred to cause it. When that man is in the employ of the Crown and therefore not someone who might easily become dishevelled, it suggests what affects him is no trifle.'

'That is not understanding it,' Crowhurst replied. 'My new, if somewhat temporary position as Her Majesty's private secretary has afforded me a status I had not expected to receive.'

Holmes frowned. 'Something untoward has happened to Sir Henry Ponsonby then?'

Colonel Crowhurst nodded. 'A boating accident. He was fortunate to survive, although he will be recovering for some time; I and another took parts of Sir Henry's workload and have been advising Her Majesty in his absence.'

'I see,' Holmes said, puffing on his pipe. 'The other is?'

'Major John Finch.'

Holmes removed his pipe from his mouth, tutted, then sat back in his chair. 'I assume, Colonel, that Scotland Yard not only failed in their investigation but they also kept you out of things, until that failure could no longer be ignored?'

Colonel Crowhurst raised an eyebrow. 'Precisely. Although how you determined an investigation of any sort has already occurred is beyond me.'

'That you are drinking tea in my sitting-room tells me, Colonel. And since it *is* you, who now acts as Sir Henry would, then clearly my advice is sought on a highly delicate matter – one that has been carefully kept out of the public eye.'

'Your reputation is well earnt,' the colonel said with a smile.

Holmes inclined his head. 'Since I've established a significant length of time has already passed, and along with it any little advantages I might have hoped for, I wonder why you'd even bother to come, unless…' Holmes trailed off; he frowned in thought for a moment. 'The only things that would make sense to me would be to discover you aren't the principal.'

Crowhurst smiled at him. 'I am not.'

Holmes's frown vanished and his features became unreadable. 'I see. Do I deduce correctly then, that the Crown sent you?'

'Her Majesty commanded I engage you,' Crowhurst replied, nodding.

'Thank you,' Holmes said, absentmindedly running the tip of his pipe along his bottom lip. 'And should I decide not to accept?'

The colonel remained expressionless. 'Is that likely?'

Sherlock Holmes contemplated the question before giving an answer. 'It must be understood that I commit myself to nothing. Nor will I take commands from anyone – regal or otherwise – until I've heard the full details,' he said, robustly adding, 'these are *my* commands.'

'And reasonable ones at that,' the old soldier answered, rather diplomatically, I thought.

'Very well then,' Holmes said, making himself comfortable in his seat.

Colonel Crowhurst turned to me and smiled. 'Dr Watson, I understand, will want to make detailed notes one expects will ultimately find their way into the public's eye – as your biographer – but I must ask that any such record be subject to my scrutiny *before* their inevitable presentations? He will, I'm sure, forgive me for seeking to ensure we attribute no subject nor statement to Her Majesty's voice without an assessment of that content made in advance.'

Before *I* could give the assurance the colonel wanted, Holmes leant forwards and pointed his pipe at him. 'Do I deduce correctly that Her Majesty's government has advised her *against* seeking counsel?'

'Fervently,' Colonel Crowhurst admitted.

Holmes again seemed satisfied by his answer and turned a smile on me. 'Watson, I'm sure, will agree to all your terms, Colonel.'

'Certainly,' I concurred.

Our visitor took a cigarette from the box before him and lit it.

'The detail, Mr Holmes, that you asked for in order to determine whether my journey back to Her Majesty should be a lone one, is simply this: a treasured jewel from the Crown's collection is missing.'

'Ah,' Holmes said. His interest captured, my friend leant forwards a little in his chair. 'You say the Crown's collection? Is this a jewel from Her Majesty's personal set, or part of the Crown Jewels held by the Keeper in the Tower of London?'

'The latter,' Colonel Crowhurst answered.

'I see. And this jewel holds greater value than others in her collection?'

'The King's Diamond – as it is called – is a rare pink diamond, Mr Holmes. The value of which has never, to my knowledge, been calculated.'

'You avoided the question,' Holmes remarked with a chuckle.

'Forgive me, it seemed superfluous,' admitted the colonel. 'The police asked me something similar. I didn't expect you to have such trivial concerns.'

Holmes shrugged. 'The police don't always ask the wrong questions, Colonel. They simply fail to deduce anything of relevance from the answers. Your explanation tells me something of importance, though. It's the theft itself that holds the greater interest.'

'To me? Certainly,' the colonel admitted, 'but not Her Majesty.'

'Thank you for that clarification. This jewel presents a personal connection to Her Majesty?'

'A deep rooted one,' Colonel Crowhurst replied, finishing his cigarette and stubbing it into the ashtray. 'In so far as it is Crown property and Her Majesty should very much like to see it returned.'

'And that is her only concern?'

'It is the only point I deem Her Majesty should be concerned by, yes,' Crowhurst answered carefully.

Holmes narrowed his eyes. 'And what is *your* concern?'

'Why, that we find the jewel, of course. It is my job to shield Her Majesty from trivialities.'

My friend held his pipe to his lip in thought for a moment. 'Tell me, Colonel, when was the King's Diamond discovered?'

'At some time in the fourteenth century.'

Holmes pointed to me, and I made a note.

'And how long has it been in the Tower?'

'A little under a week,' said Colonel Crowhurst.

'Can you give us some detail of the jewel's history?'

'I can give you a little. Her Majesty's aunt and godmother, Charlotte, the Princess Royal, later Dowager Queen of Württemberg, was gifted the King's Diamond by her father, Her Majesty's grandfather, King George III. Although it came from the royal collection, and therefore was not legally his to give away, it was not a prominent part and therefore the King's overreach was quietly ignored. Being a pink diamond, it wasn't favoured by many monarchs and evidently had remained locked in the Crown's vault for so long, hardly anyone considered his gifting it an issue. It was lost after Charlotte's death in 1828, but rediscovered in her burial vault at Ludwigsburg Palace, near Stuttgart, which was recently opened for renovation.'

'And in all that time, it has never once been set into an article?'

'No,' Colonel Crowhurst answered. 'The King's Diamond is a rough stone of approximately forty-five carats. It was apparently discovered in India, although there is absolutely no proof of that.'

'And for the last sixty years, the jewel has been buried with the Dowager Queen?'

Crowhurst nodded.

'Who knew of its existence, then?'

'The list really is a short one. Sir Henry, Her Majesty, Major Finch, the Prime Minister and the Home Secretary, and those last representatives of the Württemberg house of course.'

'Of course,' Holmes said. 'And was anything else of value robbed from this tomb?'

Colonel Crowhurst frowned slightly. 'You have a way of putting things, Mr Holmes. Aside from the King's Diamond, which was lost after its discovery there, some state papers, diaries, and other Crown artifacts were also returned to the Crown's collection. I have a record if you'd like to see it?'

Holmes removed his pipe from his lips. 'I *should* like to see it, yes. Now,' he said, his eyes firm. 'Perhaps you'll answer this. Has there been any other royal deaths recently?'

Crowhurst seemed surprised. 'No, sir, none. Why should you ask?'

'One might think the consequence of such a death would hardly escape the public eye,' Holmes mused.

Crowhurst shook his head. 'Indeed, no, there are protocols for that.'

Holmes nodded. 'That answers that. Tell me, has this jewel been stolen, Colonel, or is it simply misplaced?'

Colonel Crowhurst gave Holmes a thin smile. 'An excellent question, Mr Holmes. You appear to have a handle on the complexity of the case already.'

Holmes put down his pipe. 'You certainly have piqued my curiosity. I am aware of only one serious attempt to steal the Crown Jewels previously, and that happened centuries ago.'

'You refer, of course, to Thomas Blood?' the Queen's representative offered.

'A story with more substance than is publicly known, I feel sure,' Holmes mused.

'You are not wrong,' Crowhurst answered. 'There are many unofficial records, of course. Some suggest King Charles II commissioned Blood to steal the jewels for him. That Blood was originally sympathetic and fought for Charles I is true, and he apparently only turned Roundhead when it appeared Oliver Cromwell was going to win. There are whispers that the reason King Charles II treated Blood so reasonably after being caught was because he felt the Governor of Dublin, Lord Ormonde, was using Blood as a public scapegoat to cover for a Crown loss possibly perpetrated by Ormonde himself. Not that the establishment has ever admitted to it publicly – or even privately. Honestly, there's no telling exactly what the truth was, but one thing is certain—'

'No one has attempted to steal the Crown Jewels since?' Holmes finished.

'Correct, because no one has ever come close to matching the audacity of Colonel Blood,' said Crowhurst.

'Until now?'

'Until now,' Crowhurst admitted.

'If I interpret things correctly,' Holmes said, relighting his pipe. 'The Crown has lost a jewel from her collection, and her government, after exhausting its top investigators at Scotland Yard, has concluded that the jewel may simply have been misplaced rather than stolen?'

Colonel Crowhurst nodded.

'And the Crown does not agree with this assessment?'

'Her Majesty feels that failing to find her jewel, coupled with the embarrassment of having to admit someone actually took it in the first place, has led certain officials in government and at Scotland Yard to cover up the inadequacies of their investigators by suggesting that such an eventuality would be impossible to undertake. They have, in their collective wisdom, decided the more likely answer is closer to home. I must reluctantly agree, and therefore Her Majesty also agrees.'

'The facts seem to support this theory.' Holmes smoked for a moment, then turned his eyes back to Colonel Crowhurst. 'And the Yard assigned which inspector to the case?'

'A Tobias Gregson.'

I raised an eyebrow at Holmes, who offered me a grin in return. 'Well, that certainly answers any lingering questions we might have had, eh, Watson?'

'Indeed,' I mused. 'Gregson isn't the force's strongest investigator,' I added.

'I take it you've both had dealings with this inspector before then?'

'We have,' Holmes said, eyeing me. 'Watson's assessment is a kind and diplomatic one. Gregson is an imbecile, and whoever chose him for such a high-profile case is clearly an imbecile as well. Why the superintendent didn't assign Lestrade or Bradstreet instead is the real mystery. Both have the greater experience and skill. Gregson, it will hardly surprise you to discover, has neither.'

'Scotland Yard has closed the case, then?' I asked.

Colonel Crowhurst nodded. 'Inspector Gregson's report concluded there wasn't any evidence to support the idea that someone broke into the vault.'

'And since there's a detachment of armed guards at the Tower,' Holmes said, 'one assumes that conclusion pleased not only his superiors, but the guard commanders also?'

Crowhurst smiled. 'Proof positive, they say. The inspector's ideas *might* hold merit.'

My friend chuckled. 'Might they indeed?'

'In fact,' Crowhurst said, 'Gregson's report suggested that, as there were other items of similar sizes within the collection, ones that arguably could also have been taken at the same time and weren't—'

'That no theft occurred at all?' Holmes asked, raising his eyebrow.

'You have it, Mr Holmes,' Crowhurst muttered.

Holmes shook his head. 'Interesting. What else did Gregson conclude from his musings?'

'It's clear to me, and probably to you also, that Inspector Gregson may have been directed to come to those conclusions.'

My friend nodded. 'Yes. Placing blame on a member of the Royal household ensures a theft of this nature may never reach the public. A scandalous affair indeed.'

'Exactly. If there is no evidence of an external theft, then there is no weakness in the system. So, the Master of the Jewel Office, Major John Finch, now finds himself directed to begin an internal enquiry to recover the jewel. The situation is intolerable, Mr Holmes, because through these complications, they've unwittingly, or otherwise, contrived a reason for Her Majesty to take a direct interest in the proceedings.'

'Who directed Gregson to reach this conclusion?'

'It is my understanding that the Home Secretary made that decision,' Crowhurst replied.

'Sir Henry agreed with it?' Holmes asked.

'I cannot be sure of that.'

'But not long after it was made, Sir Henry suffered some sort of accident?'

'Well, I think the two events are unconnected,' Crowhurst remarked quickly. 'But yes, that's true.'

Holmes rubbed his lip in thought. 'It does appear to be a clever ploy from the Home Office, and by association, the Home Secretary.'

Colonel Crowhurst's expression turned hard. 'I have yet to understand the purpose behind this scheming, but one thing *is* certain. We *cannot* allow Her Majesty to take *any* position on the matter. Yet I know her well enough to say she will *not* be told to lie still over it. The potential embarrassment to the Crown is, therefore, colossal.'

'I now see why Lestrade or Bradstreet *weren't* asked to investigate,' Holmes remarked, refilling and lighting his pipe. 'It is an interesting case. And now we have explanations that lead us neatly up to your personal intervention, Colonel. But given what you've just explained, I find it hard to imagine anyone – least of all the Home Secretary – would sanction Her Majesty's request that *I* look into this matter?'

'You read the situation correctly, Mr Holmes. On advice from Sir Charles Faversham – the Prime Minister's permanent secretary – the Prime Minister cautioned Her Majesty directly from taking *any* hand in the matter. His desire is that the Home Secretary and Major Finch should continue to work together involving no other agency.'

'Which would seem reasonable, had the Home Secretary not manoeuvred Scotland Yard into suggesting the Crown's personal involvement,' Holmes suggested.

'The Queen has a will of her own, or rather an inquiring mind, and no official is ever likely to overcome it, once Her Majesty has decided.'

'I see. And you say Her Majesty has made it clear to others that she wishes to engage me directly?' Holmes asked.

Colonel Crowhurst nodded.

'And the Prime Minister and Home Secretary have both been informed?'

'They have.'

Holmes frowned in thought. 'One imagines they are less than pleased?'

'An understatement,' Crowhurst said, glancing at his pocket watch. 'But by officially extending her request, you can expect to be accorded *all* privileges, even if they're superficially given.'

'There is, of course, nothing commonplace about a jewel theft from the Tower of London; that alone captured my interest,' Holmes said, smiling. 'Add to it those other aspects you've described and our interest improves accordingly. It appears, Colonel, that Her Majesty knows how to play the game as well.'

Crowhurst shrugged. 'The Queen has excellent advisors, Mr Holmes.'

'She does indeed,' Holmes acknowledged.

The colonel then stood and clasped his lapels.

'Now that you have the details, sir. Will you accept Her Majesty's case?'

Sherlock Holmes returned to the mantle and draped his arm along it. 'Her Majesty's case has been woefully mishandled from the onset,' Holmes chastised.

'I feel it, and admit it,' Crowhurst acknowledged.

'The fact remains that a week has passed,' Holmes continued. 'Our thief has taken this jewel far away. I mean, what chance do we have of overtaking it, let alone finding it? It is beyond our reach.'

'As you say,' the colonel said, sighing. 'It *has* been too long.'

'The trail must surely be as cold as this tea by now,' Holmes remarked as he finished his cup, turning his back on the colonel to face the mantle. 'And yet... and yet...'

A flicker of hope seemed to cross the old soldier's aged brow. 'And yet, Mr Holmes?'

When Sherlock Holmes turned to face the colonel, his expression was one I'd seen many times before – suppressed excitement. 'Watson,' he said. 'Let us both change into something appropriate for an audience with Her Majesty the Queen.'

Colonel Crowhurst gave us both a satisfied grunt.

Chapter Two

'We shall welcome the inspector's help.'

'Are we not meeting Her Majesty at Buckingham Palace?' Holmes asked, as his keen eye took in the direction the cab driver had taken.

'Her Majesty is preparing to leave for Osbourne House, Mr Holmes. She is currently making a review of certain sights in London before that.'

'I see. We're to meet her at the Tower then?'

The colonel chuckled, but said nothing.

Holmes sat back in his seat. 'I understand that the King's Diamond was discovered missing the morning *after* it was locked in the display vault, correct?'

'Yes, Mr Holmes. We make an inventory twice a day. The first at six o'clock in the morning, the second at eleven in the evening.'

'What time do the guards change over?'

'Every four hours until the Tower is closed and secured – this happens at six o'clock in the evening. The night-watch change at midnight, and again at five.'

'A disruption occurs twice in that time,' Holmes said,

smiling. 'That's significant and suggestive.'

'Suggestive how?' Crowhurst asked.

'I merely commend the fact to your attention,' Holmes said, turning his eyes out of the window. He then turned back to the colonel. 'The stone was listed on the previous night's inventory?'

'It was.'

'And the alarm was raised at six the following morning, when that inventory was taken?'

Crowhurst nodded. 'Major Finch alerted the Tower Guard. They alerted me a little before eight that morning, and I informed the Queen so after.'

Holmes nodded. 'And were both inventories made by the same person?'

'No, the Jewel Office staff make those routine inventories, along with a Yeoman Warder. It was one of Major Finch's staff who performed the following morning's account.'

'I should like to have a list of all peoples who've seen or had access to the King's Diamond.'

'I had one drawn up for the inspector,' the colonel said. 'I'll have a copy made for you.'

'Now, tell me how and when the stone arrived at the Tower.'

'I brought it myself and took it directly to Major Finch around noon a week ago Thursday, after it had arrived at Buckingham Palace and been reviewed by Her Majesty.'

Holmes raised an eyebrow. 'You did?'

'That's correct. Her Majesty wanted to examine the stone, along with other Crown artifacts that came with it. I kept it at Buckingham Palace for a day.'

'And it was never unguarded?'

'Not once. It remained in my possession. No one in the household had any actual knowledge of it, and the fact it was a pink rock helped, since most people assumed it was quartz or something like that. Hardly anyone knew it was a rare diamond – we kept it that way.'

'I see,' Holmes said, nodding. 'Go on.'

'Major Finch secured it in the display vault in my presence and that of two Yeoman Warders. It was there that evening when the Warders performed the nightly inventory.'

'And was gone from the display vault at six the next morning?' Holmes muttered.

'Correct,' Crowhurst said.

'There was no visible sign of forced entry on any locks?'

The colonel shook his head.

'And no one saw anyone who shouldn't have been there, between the time the stone *had* been there?'

'That is correct.'

'I am grateful you brought this case to my attention,' Holmes said, sitting back in his chair. 'The more I hear, the more unique it appears.'

The journey wasn't long and, as Holmes predicted, we did eventually come to a stop at the Tower of London. Had we not known we were meeting Her Majesty, it would have been evident a senior member of the Royal Family was present simply by the contingent of courtiers – some prominent enough for me to recognise – along with the larger than usual military presence.

Colonel Crowhurst led us away from a gathering crowd, over a large moat that years past had formed the Tower's main defence, through the main entrance into what he referred to as, the Outer Ward. The colonel pointed out St. Thomas's Tower on our right as we passed, then directed us left to a small door, leading us through what I could describe as a secret entrance, which emerged onto a well-manicured green. After Crowhurst directed us on a brief journey past the Guard House and into Wakefield Tower – where we ascended a wide stone stair into the grand Jewel House itself – he instructed us to wait, and withdrew.

I immediately turned my attention to the stunning and mesmerising sparkle of artifacts – set, as they were on a glass-enclosed pedestal in the centre of the bright room surrounded by a thick iron gate – while we waited. It occurred to me whoever had managed to breach such security must have been very brazen and highly skilled.

Sherlock Holmes's interest, unlike mine I suspect, centred solely on the crime Crowhurst had sought to persuade him to come and solve. Despite his perceived reticence, I knew Her Majesty was in no danger of being disappointed by his declining her request. The very idea was laughable, as the case presented all the elements and circumstances which could not possibly have failed to draw his attention – I'd even go so far as to say wild horses couldn't have dragged him away from it.

For myself, I admit those objects before me held a tangible link to a system I'd been in service of, and in reverence to, my whole life. I pointed to various articles, vocalising my wonder as I did, and Holmes nodded and smiled in that polite way of his, as I waxed lyrical. Only occasionally did his eyes flick around the bright airy room – no doubt to determine how the villain had gained entry and exited with his prize. A few times I noticed his eyes fall on an alcove, where the light didn't quite reach to illuminate it, creating a dark corner. It appeared to subvert his interest, which until that point had all but been bestowed upon me. I paused my commentary to examine what he seemed fixated on, but I admit I could not see what had gained his curiosity – not until a rather diminutive and highly recognisable figure dressed almost entirely in black slipped out of the dark alcove to stand mere feet from us. Evidently, Queen Victoria had been in the room the entire time I'd been going on and on about her jewels, and Holmes had clearly known it. Well, of course he did.

'Your Majesty is an observer of people,' Holmes remarked, after we'd both shown the proper respect meeting a sovereign demanded.

'It is a pastime we aren't often afforded outside of those closest to us, Mr Holmes,' the Queen replied, turning a thin smile on me. 'Dr Watson has an exceptional knowledge of our artifacts.'

'Your Majesty is too kind,' I said, to a slight inclination of her head.

The Queen then pointed a short finger towards the display. 'You see that lone cup?' she asked me as I turned to look. 'It has been used in seven successive coronations, ours included. It is an item of unmeasured value, crafted from the finest metals and set ablaze by the purest jewels in our Empire. To the Crown, it is as precious as any of its subjects.'

'Indeed,' I ventured to say.

'It is a symbol of the institution we were ordained to rule over,' Her Majesty said, turning a whisper of a smile in my direction.

'And yet, Your Majesty,' Holmes said, his unemotional remark causing the Queen's eyes to shift from me. 'It *is* just a cup.'

I held my breath. Holmes would often be contrarian to those in authority – which seemed to be his default position – but to be so against our Queen somehow felt even more disrespectful than usual.

'Quite,' the Queen replied, and I let out my breath, for I observed the smile that tinged her otherwise expressionless face. 'A vessel only. Its value, as a commodity, is measured by its weight in gold and jewels, but its usefulness as a vessel is only good so long as it continues to hold its contents, and does not spring a leak.'

Holmes inclined his head. 'Your Majesty speaks the truth, on many levels.'

'Then may I assume you understand our predicament?'

Holmes glanced at her, then set his eyes back on the display. 'I believe I do. In order for me to investigate the problem, I must objectively review *all* who might have some connection to it.'

Queen Victoria nodded. 'Which puts us in the unenviable situation of revealing troubles within our house.' The Queen's eyes did not leave the display case.

'Your Majesty must know I will not work blind, not if it affects my ability to succeed for her.'

The Queen nodded. 'We know this of you, since you've

rather impertinently told us the same on two other occasions,' she said, but as cold as her words seemed there was a twinkle to her eye which suggested she was familiar with Holmes's methods, and that she didn't actually dislike his aloofness–rather she appeared to find some comfort in his strength. Queen Victoria turned to the display case. 'This collection of objects you see before you belongs to the Crown, and through us, it belongs to our people. The King's Diamond, I'm told, once held prominence, but like any black sheep, it lost its favour until my grandfather made a gift of it to my aunt. For that we say it was his right as sovereign and we therefore hold no annoyance over the matter. It was returned, Mr Holmes, and we rejoiced.'

'Then someone took it again,' Holmes said.

'And this we hold *great* annoyance for,' the Queen replied. 'The act of someone who has designs above their station, perhaps?'

The way Her Majesty said that made me consider if she meant something else, but I lost track of the thought as Holmes spoke. 'I believe I understand what Her Majesty is attempting to convey?'

Queen Victoria remained unreadable. 'A jewel, Mr Holmes, is nothing more than a rock. A compact ancient geological marvel, whose sparkle causes terrible choices to be made in reverence to it.' The queen turned her eyes on him. 'Something terrible has happened as a result of it, and we would seek answers for why. Since it appears we cannot rely on our government's objectivity or its subjectivity, we must, rather reluctantly, turn all our hopes on you.'

'Many jewels in Your Majesty's collection have a bloody and violent history,' Holmes said.

'Yes, we are aware, and plenty of those dark histories result from the Crown,' the Queen countered with a firm tone.

Holmes kept his eyes on the Queen. 'Perhaps I might seek an answer by looking into the stone's history? Prior to it being sealed in your aunt's tomb?'

Queen Victoria levied a smile on him. 'One imagines that

would be a useful thing to do. We recall a similar event where a grave, or tomb as you put it, had to be opened in the past. It belonged to our grandfather, the King. Perhaps that information will be of some use?'

Holmes nodded. 'Now, if I may ask. Why has Your Majesty made her request of me so public?'

The Queen tightened her jaw for a moment, then looked up at him. 'We have several reasons,' she stated, keeping her eyes affixed to his. 'All of which we believe you comprehended prior to accepting my invitation to come. Or have we misread your intellect?' Her Majesty continued to hold his gaze, and it was Holmes who broke eye contact with a slight shake of his head.

'You have not,' my friend said in reply. 'May I ask if Sir Henry would approve of your actions?'

The Queen smiled. 'He would not. But since he is currently incapacitated, we decided to take those matters into our own hands.'

'I understand.'

The Queen seemed satisfied. 'The Crown will take care of your fees, Mr Holmes, and will also allow our private secretary to assist you in any way you deem necessary, in order that you might both reach a satisfactory conclusion. We have read of your exploits through the doctor's hand and we therefore have strong hope you'll succeed where others have not.' The Queen held out her hand and Holmes took it.

'We should be delighted to receive you and your companion at Osbourne House when you have brought the affair to a conclusion.'

'I cannot guarantee the answer I bring will please you,' Holmes said, touching her hand to his nose.

For the first time, the Queen seemed genuinely amused as she clasped his hand with both of hers. 'It is fortunate, then, that unlike many of our predecessors, we do not execute bearers of bad news. I said *a* conclusion, Mr Holmes.'

Holmes briefly looked down as the Queen retracted her hands.

'We wish you success,' Queen Victoria said as she made a hand gesture which brought Colonel Crowhurst beside us. We each bowed, and the colonel saw us down to the chamber below and out of Wakefield Tower.

* * *

The warmth of the spring sun caused a gathering of crowds at the entrance, but until Her Majesty left, they would have to continue their wait. At the entrance to the Guard House, Sherlock Holmes pulled from his jacket pocket his rarely used silver cigarette case – a gift, if I recall correctly, from Queen Victoria on a previous occasion – and offered us each a smoke. Like the oddities we would soon discover in our case, this unusual sentimental act seemed equally abnormal.

Holmes had spent a few minutes in review of a map the colonel had supplied him, whilst I attempted to recall every moment of my meeting with our sovereign. Holmes, I knew, had met her several times before, but this was my first, and I was still rather in awe of it.

'I can't believe the Queen was standing in the room the entire time I went on about her artifacts,' I said, adding, 'really, Holmes, you could have said something.'

'Her Majesty was taken by you,' my friend said, looking up from his map. 'That's something for you to cheer.'

'The fact she knew who I was *and* had read some of my work definitely made my day,' I replied, lighting the smoke off a match and tossing it.

'The Queen has read every one of your stories, Doctor,' Crowhurst corrected. This revelation pleased me to no end.

Holmes uttered an amused grunt. 'And yet despite that, Watson, Her Majesty *continues* to hold you in high regard.'

'Oh, very droll, Holmes,' I murmured.

Holmes gave me a wide grin.

'Where should you like to begin?' the colonel asked, as Holmes let out an enormous cloud of smoke.

'Once Her Majesty has departed, we'll begin a review of *all* entrances into Wakefield Tower. We'll then make a second review of the display vault in the Jewel House to confirm a theory, and then we'll have a brief conversation with Major Finch.'

'You have a theory already?' I asked, somewhat surprised.

My friend turned his eyes back to his map. 'Given the scale of this crime, Watson, I have contrived of no less than four that could prove correct, given time.'

I knew it would be pointless to ask him to divulge anything at such an early stage, but Colonel Crowhurst didn't know any better. 'What are they?' he intoned.

'My little secrets for now,' replied Holmes with a wink.

Colonel Crowhurst looked at me as I shrugged. To his credit, he simply took it in his stride and nodded. 'While you were in with Her Majesty,' he said, retrieving a paper from his pocket, 'the Home Office sent through this telegram, saying that Scotland Yard has—'

'Has asked Inspector Gregson to continue to be their liaison?' said Holmes as he rolled up the map and slipped it into his pocket.

'Yes.' Crowhurst handed the telegram over. 'You expected it?'

'I thought it not unlikely they'd include him,' Holmes muttered as he read the detail.

'As a spy, you mean?' I complained.

Crowhurst's expression turned grim as he nodded at me.

'Let us not be disingenuous,' Holmes said, returning the telegram to the colonel. 'We shall welcome the inspector's help. I feel certain we might come to rely on him further down the road.'

'You cannot be serious, Holmes?'

My friend simply shrugged. 'It's not a straightforward case, Watson. That much must be obvious to you?'

'Well, the circumstances *are* out of the ordinary I'll grant you, but it *is* only a theft when you look closer at it.'

Sherlock Holmes gave me an amused smile. 'That's your assessment, is it?'

I knew my friend well enough to recognise when I was being baited. 'It was,' I admitted. 'You're suggesting there's something deeper going on, then?'

Holmes nodded. 'Deeper, murkier, sinister… perhaps. Stealing the sovereign's jewel would never be an easy task, Watson, but it would have been *far* easier, I'm sure you'll agree, to have taken it *before* it was locked in the Tower vault which has only been breached once, as we established earlier, and long before modern security arrangements were put in place to make it almost impossible – and is guarded at all hours of the day by twenty-two heavily armed members of Her Majesty's Tower Guard, plus a contingent of Yeoman Warders, and the Tower staff. And, if that wasn't enough, it's apparently a rare *pink* diamond, which hardly anyone would recognise *as* a diamond.'

'Now that you put it that way, it seems rather difficult,' I mused.

'Difficult? It's ridiculous,' Holmes said with a snort.

'You don't think it was stolen, do you?' Colonel Crowhurst asked him, a frown forming on his aged face.

Holmes smiled. 'Oh, it was stolen, Colonel, of that, I am convinced.'

Crowhurst's frown deepened. 'Then…?'

Holmes waved a hand. 'We must cease speculating and deal with facts only from this point forwards. The facts as we know them tell us the King's Diamond was secured in the display vault on Thursday around noon, where it remained until eleven that same evening – and sometime between then and six of the following morning, it had gone.'

'Succinctly put,' the colonel said.

'It was guarded at all times?'

'It was,' the colonel agreed.

'I therefore suggest, given the security, it is improbable that an unknown agent could have gone anywhere near the Jewel House unchallenged.'

Colonel Crowhurst, it appeared, may have already reached a similar conclusion, since he did not seem surprised by it.

'But not impossible?' I asked.

Holmes smiled. 'Not impossible, no. Improbable. Given what we know, might we conclude that someone with prior knowledge of this long-missing jewel came here to steal it?' Holmes asked, looking between us.

'An inside man?' I suggested.

Holmes turned to Crowhurst. 'It would answer how they knew what to take – since they took nothing else. What's your assessment, Colonel?'

'As much as I hate to admit it, I think you and Dr Watson might have hit on the truth.'

Holmes lit another cigarette, then turned his eyes on us both. 'And neither of you can conceive of any other theory which might fit the facts?'

Crowhurst glanced at me before we both turned and shook our heads.

Sherlock Holmes seemed satisfied. 'Then we shall proceed with this as our theory and investigate accordingly.'

'Should we not wait for the inspector to arrive before starting?' Crowhurst asked.

My friend shook his head. 'That would be neither useful nor necessary. Gregson has made his review and is unlikely to form any new opinions a second time – at least none that I'm interested in hearing.' Holmes dropped his cigarette and extinguished it with his shoe. 'Ah, splendid,' he said, lifting his cane and pointing. 'If I am not mistaken, that is Her Majesty's carriage passing Byward Tower?'

'It is,' Colonel Crowhurst replied. 'And off to Portsmouth for her crossing to Osbourne House.'

'Excellent,' Holmes said. 'Then if you gentlemen have no objection, I should very much like to begin.'

Chapter Three

'Has Mother Time beaten the celebrated Mr Sherlock Holmes?'

On entering the chamber room of the Jewel House, Holmes instructed us to stand to one side, and he immediately leapt into work. My friend had a very methodical approach to most things, and as I had spent several years observing his methods, I could see how the routine of his examination of this room did not differ from any previous one I'd been witness to. Only when he came upon those interesting articles that might give him some vital clue did he pause, but otherwise for the next twenty minutes he poured over everything and anything that might give him the answer he sought – and when Holmes finally stood staring at the display case, his glass replaced by a cigarette, I recognised when it would be acceptable to approach him. I tapped Colonel Crowhurst's arm, and we both came alongside him.

'What can you tell us, Mr Holmes?' Crowhurst asked.

'Very little,' my friend replied. 'There has been so much traffic since, one cannot know what might be evidence or not.'

'I am sorry,' Crowhurst murmured.

'Fortunately, I had pinned little hope of discovering

anything of significant value,' my friend said. 'Certainly not at this stage of my investigation.'

Crowhurst seemed, if I might say, a little disappointed in Holmes. Although he tried to put on the reserved mantle of a man who recognised what 'too much time has passed' might mean to an investigation, he appeared restless and maybe unsettled by my friend's lack of revelations. I, however, felt no such uncertainty, for I had picked up on his use of a single word. A word which gave me hope where clearly the colonel saw none. Holmes had said he'd not discovered anything of *significant* value.

'But you've been able to corroborate *something*? A theory or two, perhaps?' I said, putting my emphasis on the word something. Holmes offered me that rarest of smiles which told me I'd made an accurate assessment of his statement.

'Perhaps,' was all he would say, but the sparkle in his eyes told me so much more. He then turned to the colonel. 'I think it time we spoke with Major Finch, don't you?'

Colonel Crowhurst led us to Major Finch's office, where we sat with a fresh pot of tea between us. Finch was a thin man who was a little shy of six-feet tall. He had a thick but short brushed black beard, and on top of a great beak of a nose sat the smallest pair of pince-nez I had ever seen. Holmes and Finch went over most of what he and Crowhurst had discussed already. In an effort, I rather suspected, to ensure the robustness of the facts Holmes had already gathered. Once Holmes seemed satisfied, he sat in a chair and sipped his tea in contemplation.

'What do you make of it, Mr Holmes?' asked Major Finch. 'It's a terrible business.'

'Terrible,' Crowhurst muttered, his cup paused at his lips. He shook his head and then took a long slurp. 'Mr Holmes may have been thwarted by time.'

'Thanks to that wretched policeman,' Finch growled in agreement.

My friend continued to drink his tea in quiet, and

Crowhurst and Finch recognised he wasn't fully engaged, so turned their attention to him.

'Do you have any theories, sir?' Major Finch asked. 'Has Mother Time beaten the celebrated Mr Sherlock Holmes?'

Holmes placed his cup carefully into the saucer and then smiled. 'I have one,' he said.

Finch and Crowhurst looked at each other. But it was the colonel who spoke first. 'Just the one?'

'Just one,' Holmes reiterated. 'It occurs to me' – he placed the cup and saucer on the side-table and leant forwards in his chair – 'only a select few people had access to this jewel, prior to its coming to Buckingham Palace.'

'That's true, Mr Holmes. It came in secret under an official decree. The stone wasn't even listed in the manifest, only in a letter to Her Majesty, which was passed to me from Sir Henry.'

'Then only you, Sir Henry, and Her Majesty knew of it,' Holmes mused. 'Until you called for the Queen's Jeweller to come to the palace?'

'However did you know I did that?' Crowhurst asked. 'It's true, I called on Major Finch to come, because—'

'Well, of course you did,' Holmes interrupted. 'The Queen's Jeweller *must* be present when someone returns a lost diamond of such value to her?'

Colonel Crowhurst seemed surprised by the interruption. 'Why, yes, of course.'

'One imagines,' said Holmes, 'this was done to validate the authenticity of the claim?'

'Indeed,' Crowhurst replied, looking to Finch, who gave a slight shrug. 'Although we had no reason to doubt it *was* the King's Diamond,' he added.

'No reason?' Holmes laughed. 'You had every reason. An uncut pink diamond is so rare,' Holmes continued. 'You could not take such a claim on face value, surely?'

'Well, no—'

'Someone in Her Majesty's court would have *insisted* an expert come to verify that it wasn't, say, a chunk of abundantly common rose quartz?'

'Exactly right,' Major Finch said, nodding. 'And, at Sir Henry's request—'

Holmes held up a hand, cutting him off. 'That all seems clear, Major.'

My friend stood and paced the room for a moment before coming to a decision. 'There are several challenges,' he said. 'The head start our thief has on us must surely be the biggest of them all.'

Major Finch glanced at Crowhurst, then sighed. 'So, it *is* down to time, then?'

'That would not be an unreasonable analysis,' Holmes said. He then smiled. 'Still, there *is* hope. We have no reason to suspect, after a week has passed, the stone has left the thief's hands.'

This information seemed to pique Major Finch's curiosity as he seemed much more attentive.

'Because no one has tried to sell it,' Crowhurst said, nodding.

Holmes laughed. 'Oh, my dear colonel. They have already sold it.'

'But,' Crowhurst spluttered, 'who would buy it?' It was apparent he did not believe this was possible. 'A Crown artifact, Mr Holmes, would be recognised all over the world.'

My friend, however, turned his eyes on Major Finch. 'Is that so, Major?'

Major Finch shook his head. 'Sorry to contradict you, Colonel, but no. It's been in the archive record, of course, and many people know something of it, but those records are fragmented. There are no drawings or etchings of the Crown's collection, in printed form privately or publicly, that have the King's Diamond in them, as far as I know.'

'Is that because it was hidden for thirty years?' I asked.

'True, but even before that,' Finch replied. 'Although prominent in the Crown's collection, Doctor, it wasn't given a spotlight since nearly all reigning monarchs considered it the lesser piece.'

'There you have it,' Holmes said, spreading his hands out.

'Mother time hast maketh fools of all.'

Finch gave a deep sigh.

'Then we must inform Her Majesty, Mr Holmes,' Colonel Crowhurst said unhappily.

Holmes smiled, then extended his hand. 'Before we do that, I'd ask Major Finch first to place Her Majesty's diamond into my hand,' my friend said expectantly. 'That way we might close off this little affair before lunch and get on with our respective lives. You, of course, Major, will be left answering the more difficult of any questions. What do you say?'

Colonel Crowhurst and I stared at Holmes as he held Major Finch under his scrutiny. The major, having been outed by Holmes, initially laughed, but seeing the stern expression of my friend, with his hand still extended, the major knew he'd been outsmarted. Without a second thought, he picked up the teapot and threw the liquid into Holmes's face, but my friend covered it with his hand, and the hot liquid splashed harmless against his jacket and arm. The distraction was enough to ensure the major could displace the table and chairs between us, kicking Crowhurst's chair over and depositing him at Holmes's feet, still holding his teacup, allowing Finch to escape the room.

'After him, Watson!' Holmes bellowed as he helped Crowhurst to his feet.

When I'd clambered over the upturned furniture and made it out of the room, I discovered Major Finch was nowhere to be seen.

'The cunning devil had his plan of escape worked out from that room,' Holmes mused. 'I had thought bringing him here would ease his suspicions, but he has far more intelligence than I'd credited him for.'

'What is all this?' Crowhurst asked, still – it amused me to note – holding his teacup. 'Major Finch is involved in this affair?'

Holmes took the colonel by the shoulders, then looked into his eyes. 'Watson, the colonel might have hit his head.'

I immediately took the cup from him and checked. 'Yes, there's a slight bump here. Perhaps you should sit down for a moment?'

Crowhurst waved me away. 'Stop fussing. What is going on here?'

'We have no time for this,' Holmes declared, scanning the corridor briefly before dashing off.

'How in the world did you know about Finch?' Crowhurst breathed, as he and I attempted to keep up with Holmes, who continued his run down long corridors, stopping on occasions to peer out of a window.

'Explanations can come later,' Holmes commanded. 'There,' he yelled, excitedly pointing.

'Stop that man!' Colonel Crowhurst's robust voice added to our own as several guards came to our calls for help, and in understanding, took up the chase for us.

Holmes took in the view for a moment, consulting a rather detailed map of the Tower he'd obviously brought with him – his eyes darting back and forth. 'The fellow knows this place better than anyone,' he said with a curse. 'We'll be hard pressed to catch him now.'

'He can't get far!' yelled Crowhurst. 'We'll catch the fellow.'

* * *

'Major Finch had his escape planned out in advance,' Holmes remarked an hour later, as we made a slow walk back to the Jewel Keeper's office, after checking in with the front entrance guards. As we approached the green, Holmes slowed, and we all stopped and shared a smoke.

'He can't escape the Tower though,' Crowhurst growled for possibly the fifth or sixth time. 'No, sir. Not without a boat.'

'I don't think we need concern ourselves with that for the moment. The Major won't leave the Tower. His actions tell me he's intelligent and clearly has a motive we've yet to understand.'

'How can you be so sure of that?' Crowhurst asked.

'He chose to remain,' Holmes pointed out. 'Even after knowing I would come.'

'You suggest there's something more going on here?' Crowhurst asked him.

'I am of that opinion, yes. Finch can lie low within the Tower's interconnected tunnels and rooms for days. He can remain a step ahead of us.'

'Then we will employ the men to search the Tower.'

Holmes chuckled. 'The odds are still in his favour. I suspect Finch has gone to a place pre-fortified with weapons *and* food, and if my reasoning is correct, he needs time to consider things – which in effect grants us the same.'

'But *why* do you say he won't leave?' Crowhurst asked.

My friend was thoughtful. 'It seems to me he has a mission and I suspect he won't leave until it is completed.'

'What mission? What *is* all this about?' There was an edge in Crowhurst's voice that made Holmes nod.

'My apologies, Colonel. I recognise it *is* rather past the time for explanations, but I beg you indulge me just a smidgen further.'

'I appear to have little choice,' the colonel said.

Holmes nodded at him. 'Now, what we could do with are a few more men.'

'Then *they* should please you,' Colonel Crowhurst said, waving enthusiastically at a cadre of uniformed policemen who had just entered through the main gate, led by Inspector Gregson.

'I told you we'd need his help,' Holmes remarked, chuckling at me as we waited for the inspector to reach us.

Gregson extended his hand to Holmes. 'A little bird tells me, Mr Holmes, that the culprit was right under your nose,' he said, shaking his hand. 'And that you let him escape?' There was humour in his voice that caused Holmes to let out a chuckle.

'He was under *your* nose, too, Gregson,' Holmes said, tapping his chest. 'Or had you forgotten that?'

'That's fair, Mr Holmes,' the old inspector said. 'So, you've had no sign since he ran?'

'None,' Crowhurst said. 'We don't think he's left yet, either.'

'You believe he's still here, do you?'

'Mr Holmes does, yes,' I said. The inspector looked around for a moment, then Holmes took his arm.

'We're about to head back to his office,' Holmes said. 'Join us, won't you?'

Inspector Gregson nodded, gave instructions to his officers, who then joined the uniformed guards searching for Major Finch, and we all followed Holmes back to the Jewel Keeper's rooms.

* * *

Sherlock Holmes walked to the window and lit a cigarette. 'I suppose I couldn't decide at first *why* the jewel had been moved to the Tower at all, but then Her Majesty alluded to the scandal of her potentially ousting a member of her family over the theft, and that's when it occurred to me the major might have somehow been involved.'

Colonel Crowhurst sank into his chair. 'I have been utterly blind!'

'Tell me, Mr Holmes,' Gregson asked, eyeing the Queen's servant, 'how you could be sure it was Finch, and not the colonel here?'

Crowhurst gaped at him.

'Colonel Crowhurst could have taken the jewel from the palace,' Holmes replied.

'So, the stone was always *meant* to be taken from the Tower?' I asked.

Holmes nodded. 'Yes. That appears to be a key component to this affair. It had to be done here.'

'Given the security arrangements then, it seems obvious there had to be an insider,' I pointed out. 'One cannot simply take a jewel from Her Majesty's display, no matter how prepared they came. The only way that could happen is if the person who took it was also the person with access to it.'

'Bravo, my dear fellow,' Holmes said. 'It was obvious to me that as none of those formidable locks were forced, nor were any left unopened, someone must have used a key to open it, then carefully locked it up again.'

'And that's why you outed Finch?'

Holmes winked at me. 'It was one of the reasons. The nature of this theft must surely seem a little curious to the rest of you, no?'

We all looked at each other, but it was Crowhurst who asked. 'Such as?'

Holmes smiled at him. 'It was clear that whoever took this piece cared enough to ensure no others were touched. I find that remarkable, and telling.'

'I always assumed it was no opportunistic theft,' Inspector Gregson said. 'It was always possible that an insider with keys could have done it. I assumed it was someone with the ability to take anything from that display, and the ability to remain above reproach and suspicion. But we cannot go around accusing senior members of Her Majesty's household of stealing her jewels. Not without evidence,' the inspector pointed out.

Holmes nodded. 'And had you made an examination of Finch's person, as I did, you would have had that evidence. Did anyone take the time to examine his knees and elbows?'

'No,' Crowhurst said.

'Nor I,' I replied.

'Ah, well, had you done so, you would have seen evidence that he had recently been on those knees and elbows, in somewhere damp and filthy – given how meticulous his dress was, and how his work is unlikely to see him crawling through dark tunnels, it seemed pretty clear he'd been engaged in something outside of his current duties for a while. Possibly a week?'

'You came up with all that just by an examination of the displays and his knees?' Crowhurst asked.

Holmes smiled at him. 'I determined a little in Baker Street. I simply needed the data to corroborate it.'

'Well,' the colonel said, glancing at Gregson. 'One wonders *why* the police didn't see it?'

'On the contrary,' my friend said before Gregson could reply. 'I think the inspector *did* see it, and if I am correct,' Holmes said smiling, 'there're men at Finch's address as we speak?'

Inspector Gregson inclined his head. 'That is correct, Mr Holmes.'

'Good lord!' Crowhurst muttered. 'Am I the *only* one in the dark here?'

'Not the only one,' I muttered.

'I recognised the tactic when the colonel explained it to me,' Holmes said to Gregson. 'You couldn't be sure if the King's Diamond was still here, so you let Finch know the matter was being dropped in favour of an internal investigation.'

'Which put him at ease knowing the police weren't looking at him?' I offered. 'That's clever.'

'It was the superintendent's plan,' Gregson said.

'Meaning the Home Secretary was in on it?' Crowhurst asked, apparently shocked by the revelation.

Gregson nodded. 'We'd concluded, as Mr Holmes had, that Finch was the only person who could have taken it. And everything was going fine until we were told of Mr Holmes's involvement. The superintendent dispatched me at once to the Tower, as he was worried Mr Holmes's appearance might upend our investigation – and it seems he wasn't wrong.'

Holmes turned a look on the inspector. 'Well, after a week of surveillance, one assumes if you'd had *anything* to arrest him for, Finch would have been in custody long before I arrived.'

'He's a slippery fellow,' Gregson muttered. 'But you're correct, Mr Holmes. We have nothing. We've kept a record of his movements, and descriptions of anyone who has been to his house. My question now is, how does he hope to escape?'

'If my estimation of his intelligence is accurate, he has

already made an escape – but has since returned.'

Gregson shook his head. 'Someone would have seen him,' he said.

'Someone undoubtably saw him,' Holmes scoffed.

'I don't see how that's possible,' Gregson said. 'With all these uniforms looking for him, no… it's simply a matter of time before we find him. He's got quite a distinctive look.'

Holmes chuckled. 'Ah yes, the fellow does have a thick black beard. Not one of you thought it might have been a disguise?'

'Why should we? Finch has *always* worn a beard of that type,' Crowhurst pointed out.

'And yet, none of you noticed he'd recently shaved it off and replaced it with a false one.'

'Well how could we have!' Crowhurst grumbled.

'Forgive me,' Holmes said. 'I do tend to look harder at people with thick black beards.'

We said nothing.

'Well, Inspector, are you *still* convinced you'll find him? Care to place a wager on it?' Sherlock Holmes said flippantly. 'A gold sovereign says you won't, no matter how many men you have.'

'Well, I'll grant you with that beard off, it *might* be a little more difficult, but how are *you* so sure you'll find him then?' the inspector growled.

'Because I have not failed to recognise that Major Finch is a far cleverer adversary than you or anyone else here has given him credit for,' Holmes replied. 'He laid the plans for his escape in advance, yet did not feel the need to abscond even after the police were called in. I postulate he was aware of your surveillance, but even if he wasn't, his actions suggest he expected to be put under scrutiny and acted accordingly.'

'Meaning he's played all of us, including you?' Gregson asked.

'Yes,' Holmes replied. 'Including me.'

'Wait a moment,' I said, interrupting their conversation. 'You said Finch had made an escape *and* subsequently returned? Yet earlier you said he *can't* leave. I don't understand that.'

'Nor I,' Crowhurst said, latching onto my thought.

Holmes smiled. 'Well, I suppose it would be more accurate to say Finch won't leave for long periods. He might have slipped away to pass a message onto a confederate, but he'll have returned quickly enough.'

Inspector Gregson frowned. 'You're suggesting there's a conspiracy here?'

'I'm *not* suggesting it,' Holmes said as he lit his pipe. 'There *is* a conspiracy, Inspector.'

'Well, that's *your* idea,' the inspector said, sighing. 'How can you be so sure?'

Holmes shrugged. 'I simply observed Major Finch had the opportunity to take any artifact he wanted from the Crown's display case – and yet he chose one that had just arrived and hardly anyone knew anything about. It *is* suggestive.'

'Of what?' I asked.

'That Finch has a reason to want to keep us all here,' Holmes said.

'I don't see how that makes any difference,' Gregson grumbled.

'Don't you, Inspector?' Holmes asked, the twinkle in his eye unmistakable. 'You can think of no explanation for his actions?'

'A thief is a thief. He wanted the money,' Gregson offered. 'He took the one item, as you said, that no one would recognise – possibly hoping no one would notice it was missing. Also, something of importance, a fence might recognise the other items in that collection, and refuse to work on them.'

Holmes nodded. 'Finch is no ordinary thief, Inspector. And let us be clear. Given how he was so careful to ensure no other items in Her Majesty's collection could have been molested, it is reasonable to conclude he has no intention of taking that stone to any petty bottom-feeder jewel fence. What could they do with something as large as the King's Diamond? No legitimate London jeweller would take it either, since any jeweller of that calibre would require a legitimacy that would tolerate little scrutiny. There are, in fact, very few people in London capable of working on a diamond of that size and value. So, where could he take it?'

'Abroad?' I asked.

Gregson nodded. 'A legitimate jeweller outside of England, who would recognise the object's value but also be able to work on it without fear of being caught by anyone here, would be preferable. Do we think Finch would know of such a person?'

'He's the Jewel Keeper in the Tower of London. The Queen's Jeweller,' I said. 'Of course he would!'

'Good God, it's worse than we thought,' Crowhurst bellowed.

'It is not easy to arrange the removal of a jewel this prominent, unless he had a buyer already?' the inspector mused.

Holmes raised an eyebrow at him.

Gregson appeared to catch his meaning. 'He had help then?'

'He had help,' Holmes said through puffs of smoke. 'I doubt Finch woke up one morning and said, "My, that's a pretty pink diamond, I think I'll just help myself to it." No, there was a plan for it. He could have taken anything he wanted, and at any time. He had access to the *entire* Crown collection. So why didn't he?'

'That is an excellent question,' Gregson remarked. 'These others he's involved with must be the courier and seller then.'

'That certainly fits your reasoning,' Holmes said.

'Then all they need now is the jewel,' I stated.

'But you've scuppered his plans,' Crowhurst said, 'by ousting him. Surely he won't remain to be arrested? He'll need to escape too?'

'As I said before. Finch has a reason for wanting us all to remain here.'

'Because his buyer wasn't available, probably. But that leads me to ponder another question then,' Gregson said. 'Why would Finch take the jewel before he needed to? The alarm was raised, yet as you say, it appears to have been done before he was ready to enact the plan for removing it.'

Holmes nodded. 'Excellent, Inspector. *Why* take it before it was ready to be taken?'

'Well, what does that matter? The man turned scoundrel for what?' Crowhurst asked. 'Money?'

'I don't believe money plays any part in the motivation for this crime,' Holmes said. 'Because there are other questions that point to something deeper.'

'The King's Diamond was taken deliberately, then, and not on a whim?' Gregson asked.

Holmes nodded. 'Yes, and we must discover the motive behind its theft.'

'Do you think Finch plans to cut the diamond up?' Crowhurst asked – clearly the idea mortified him.

'He? Probably not. His employer – for want of a better term – might have that as a future goal. If only to make it impossible to recognise later,' Holmes said.

'Oh, good Lord,' Crowhurst moaned. 'We must prevent that at all cost!'

Holmes smiled. 'I feel certain that the stone is safe, for now.'

'How so,' Crowhurst asked.

'Well, for one thing,' Holmes said, taking the pipe from his mouth and pointing the stem at him. 'I have good reason to suspect it is still here.'

'How can you be sure?' I asked.

'Finch remained in situ until I exposed him. He considers himself the guardian of this jewel.'

'And that's the reason why he cannot leave,' the inspector said smiling. 'Because he *must* recover it before *we* do.'

Crowhurst gave a grim-faced nod.

Holmes said nothing as he smoked, electing I assumed to allow the inspector to form his own ideas. When a few minutes had passed, and Gregson and Crowhurst had all but talked themselves out, Holmes turned to the colonel. 'You said in

Baker Street you had paperwork that came along with this diamond. I wonder if I might see that?'

The colonel nodded. 'Is there anything more we can do?'

Holmes thought for a moment. 'Is the entourage of Her Majesty at Osbourne House the same as those present on the day the King's Diamond arrived?'

'Aside from the Prince of Wales, yes,' Crowhurst said. 'The Prince is in Germany.'

'Did the Prince play any part in the diamond's recovery from the Queen's aunt?'

Crowhurst shook his head.

'Then I think we might not bother the Prince regarding it.'

The colonel nodded. 'I'll have a list of everyone present drawn up for you today.'

'I'll need the records your people gathered on Finch, too, Inspector,' Holmes reminded him.

'You'll have them.'

'Then let us find a strategic place to set up our headquarters,' the colonel said. 'The guard room is fairly central and would seem an ideal choice, do you agree, Mr Holmes? Inspector?'

Holmes nodded. 'If it pleases you, then set up camp there.'

The inspector appeared to have no opinion on the matter. When Crowhurst looked to him for a reply, he simply gesticulated an affirmation with his hand.

'Excellent. We shall make preparations for dinner then.'

Holmes fixed his eyes out the window. 'We'll be along soon, Colonel.'

The inspector leant against the old stone doorway and nodded as Crowhurst passed him. 'Snooty old codger,' he mumbled somewhat unkindly. 'D'you think Finch is the only conspirator in the tower?' Gregson asked Holmes.

My friend turned to him. 'Do you?'

'No.'

Holmes gave a satisfied nod.

'So, we either find him or the jewel, then?'

'You make it sound easy, Inspector,' Holmes remarked

stoically. 'You've forgotten, perhaps, that Major Finch *has* the advantage.'

Gregson frowned. 'How so?'

'He knows where the jewel is,' I answered.

The inspector rubbed his chin. 'Right. Then we'll have to find *him* first. But where do we start, eh?'

'By reviewing the facts, and coming to a logical set of next steps.'

'*Thinking*, you mean?' Gregson said shaking his head. 'I'm all for *doing*,' he added.

'By all means, Inspector. Feel free to be doing something, but I'll say it again, it won't help you much.'

'But it might make me feel better,' the inspector said.

Holmes raised his eyebrow at me, offered a brief smile to the inspector, then collected his cane and top hat. 'Come, Watson,' said Holmes. 'I require a breath of fresh air before we formulate our next plan of action.'

Chapter Four

'Those footprints were not there earlier.'

I followed Holmes out of one of the many Tower vestibules we'd visited that day – I had lost track of which one – and into the mid-morning spring air. My friend did not seem as anxious as I might have expected. Indeed, his posture and movement said to me he wasn't expecting any further trouble, nor perhaps any further news that might speed things along. We stopped at a small stone wall and Holmes sat and took his pipe out, stuffing it from his pouch. I preferred to stand and watch the ravens as they fluttered around. The starkness of the old site made ever more eerie by the story told of those ravens and how their presence is believed to protect the Crown and the Tower; a superstition that holds "if the Tower of London ravens are lost or fly away, the Crown will fall and Britain with it." An old superstition that stands very little scrutiny. The truth is, sadly, a lot less interesting. The birds are a group of captive ravens, resident at the Tower, and their characteristic squawk I've recently learnt is often used as a call to predators after they've discover a sick or dying animal – a behaviour which seems advantageous to all concerned and somewhat indicative of our current situation. I unconsciously cast my eyes upwards lest I saw Major Finch looking down from some slit-window in one of those old towers, crying out to some unseen foe ready to attack us.

Holmes remained in quiet contemplation, smoking behind me, and after dismissing those black thoughts, I turned my eyes back to the ravens, losing myself in the imagery of the majestic creatures poking around on the lawn ahead of me. I became so enwrapped in their movements, I failed to hear Holmes speak, but his touch on my shoulder quickly drew my attention.

'Sorry,' I said, 'did you say something?'

'I simply asked what it was you were contemplating,' he said, tapping his pipe out. 'Although seeing those furtive glances of yours darting around the place, I suppose I hardly needed to ask.' Holmes chuckled as he refilled his pipe.

'No, I suppose not. Have you come up with a plan?' I asked, sitting on the wall and lighting a cigarette.

'Not yet.' Holmes continued to clean his pipe. 'I fear it might turn into a very dull afternoon for you, my dear fellow.'

I smiled. 'I suppose it can't always be a good chase down a corridor.'

'For now, at least, that is so.'

'Was Inspector Gregson wrong about wanting to be doing… something?'

Holmes shrugged. 'Until you know what to look for, it seems a rather pointless thing to do – much like a lot of police work, in fact.'

I sighed at Holmes's misnomer regarding policing, but kept those thoughts to myself. 'I do feel rather useless just, well, sitting here – especially when Finch is here *somewhere*. Sorry, Holmes, I think I agree with Gregson. A co-ordinated search *must* eventually find him.'

'Under normal circumstances, I would agree. But this situation is far from normal. And I should point out, this is a game of cat and mouse. Wherever we move to, Finch will have vacated ahead of time.'

'Because he can see us coming?' I flicked my eyes upwards

again.

'Precisely. The layout of the Tower offers many advantages to Major Finch, and his knowledge of the various less known and perhaps secret entrances and exits will, as I did previously caution, keep him one step ahead. What is required now is logic, order, and a little carefully orchestrated method.'

'So, what must we do?'

'Firstly, we must convince Crowhurst to position men at each tower window. They offer us a restricted view of the grounds, of course, but one or other *might* get a glimpse of Finch's movement.'

I nodded. 'That's an excellent idea. It'll give his men some idea where to bear down on.'

'Indeed. And it should help keep them out of my way.'

'I don't understand?'

Holmes shrugged. 'It's a fool's errand, but a necessary one. We *must* allow Finch to recover the jewel, then and only then can we make our next move – and we can *only* do that once the path for him is free, do you see?'

'Not really. I mean, without knowing where he's hidden it–'

'There are difficulties,' he acknowledged. 'But then—'

'There are always difficulties, yes, I've heard you say that before.'

'It does give one an appreciation for the chase, though,' my friend said with a wink. He then chuckled at the loud rumble that emanated from my stomach. 'Lunch, my dear fellow!'

I followed Holmes into the guardroom where Colonel Crowhurst had organised quite a feast for us. We met inside and he introduced the captain of the Tower Guards, along with the head Yeoman Warder – or Beefeater, as they are more commonly referred to. Inspector Gregson stood to one side, a mug of tea in his hand and a half-eaten sandwich on the table in front of him.

I helped myself to some tea whilst Holmes chatted to Crowhurst and the other two uniforms. As I sipped my brew, savouring the tart, strong flavour, Gregson shuffled in beside me.

'Civilians aren't given the same courtesies as those military types, eh, Doctor?'

I chuckled. 'You forget, *I* am an ex-Army officer, Inspector.'

Gregson rolled his eyes and sighed. 'Well, *I* have my own men, and my own way of using them – and these fellows with their fancy uniforms might have a place of point in this old tower, but in criminal matters, they have *no* jurisdiction above mine.'

I watched, with hidden amusement, how Gregson imperiously took his lapel with his free hand as he made his speech, but as comical as he appeared, he had a point.

'So, why aren't you telling them that?' I asked.

Gregson put his mug down hard on the table, allowing a small amount of its contents to spill over the sides onto his hand, which he quickly wiped on his trousers. 'Maybe now Mr Holmes is here, I will.'

I laughed inwardly as the inspector awkwardly attempted to insert himself into their conversations. It was clear Crowhurst and the other military men had no time for him, but to my surprise it was Holmes who ultimately sided *with* Gregson, particularly on his understanding of criminal law and who would have jurisdiction, and despite Holmes's antipathy for military men, he brokered a peace between them. I selected a sandwich just as Holmes appeared beside me. He poured himself a mug of the powerful brew and turned his back to the table, observing the three men as they continued to make preparations.

'That was generous of you,' I murmured.

'It suits my purposes to have them working together, but in a way that keeps them clear of anything of consequence, and with Gregson calling the shots, we'll be sure of it.'

'What about Finch? How are the men taking his betrayal?'

'Largely as you'd expect, since you have that same mindset.'

'I understand them, having served.'

'These military people see Finch's actions as more than betrayal. It's treason for them, and as far as they're concerned, he's breached a sacred trust that should never have been broken. Honestly, Watson. It would be comical, were it not so serious.'

'And I wouldn't want to be in Finch's shoes if that captain found him before anyone else, that's for sure,' I said.

Holmes nodded. 'You aren't wrong.'

'It's because they'll take his actions far more personally, something Gregson won't understand.'

'Which is why putting Gregson in charge of these military drones is preferable.'

'Because we have a better chance of finding Finch *and* the jewel with Gregson leading?' I asked.

'Well, certainly finding Finch before anyone else,' Holmes murmured. 'Had the captain got his way, he would almost certainly have upset my ideas. Despite being blind to anything but Her Majesty's military, he's actually very intelligent.'

'Gregson has agreed to put *all* the men, his and the military's, in the towers as you hoped?'

Holmes nodded. 'Once I'd helped insert him as the authority of the law, he agreed to everything I recommended. Much to the Guard Captain's annoyance – the look I read from him was one of surprise and disappointment at my actions.'

'I'm sure his opinion of you will change once you've solved the case,' I offered.

'I have no interest in his opinion of me, nor do I care if it changes or not. The *only* thing I care about is ensuring the imbecile Gregson is calling the shots.'

I chuckled. 'You *are* terrible.'

'Maybe so,' Holmes replied, matching my levity. 'But I need Finch to see that Gregson is leading the investigation. It's imperative, Watson.'

'Why is that so important?' I asked, lifting my hand to add, 'Aside from the fact that he's less impressionable than the military. You said yourself that he's out of his depth in an investigation of this type.'

'Out of his depth, yes. An excellent analogy. But to answer your question, *Major* Finch knows these military men, and he also knows their tactics – for he trained in those tactics too. He's one of them. There might be someone in the guards that could conceivably help him – indeed, there is every reason to suspect he *is* being helped by someone. But he knows nothing about Gregson, so we play *that* game. We allow the inspector to decide things. The military hotheads will buck against him, but ultimately they'll follow because they currently have no choice.'

'I know I'm being terribly dim, but I still don't see what that gets us?'

'I still have not discerned his true motives,' Holmes said. 'Why is he keeping us here? What possible reason would he need to?'

'For the reasons Gregson said,' I reminded him. 'He needs time for his buyer—'

Holmes chuckled and I frowned. 'You mean, that wasn't true?' I asked, somewhat surprised. 'You appeared to agree with him when he suggested it.'

'That's not entirely true,' Holmes pointed out. 'I simply didn't disagree.'

'Well *now* I'm even more confused.'

'Understandably so. With luck, my plan to put Gregson in charge lulls the major into making a mistake – and one is all I'll need.'

I understood. 'How long, do you think, before Colonel Crowhurst tires of no results and overrules Gregson?'

Holmes smiled. 'A few hours, maybe longer. But I think I have an idea how we can decrease the odds of that happening.'

'Do tell,' I chuckled.

'In good time.'

'And once Finch is free to move around, that's when we'll catch him and bring him to justice?'

Sherlock Holmes took a long sip of his tea before answering, and when he finished, I noticed he kept the cup covering his lips. 'No,' he remarked softly. 'I plan to let him go.'

Recognising Holmes had said that with no intention of allowing anyone but me to hear, I kept the surprise of his statement from my voice. 'So, you *do* have a plan, then?'

My friend smiled, then drained his cup. 'The beginnings of one.'

'Can we go somewhere private so I might hear it?'

Holmes pointed at my stomach. 'Eat first,' he said, 'otherwise anywhere we do go will afford us little privacy, especially if we're to be given away by that grumbling stomach of yours.' Holmes then re-joined the others.

I dutifully collected and ate another sandwich.

* * *

It was perhaps thirty minutes later when Holmes and I were once again walking across the green away from the guardroom. The police constables and military men, including the Warders and the remaining members of Major Finch's staff – who I noticed were rightly paired with a constable – were all moving to their respective positions. The lead Warder had informed the entrance staff the Tower was closed to the public for the foreseeable future, and now the hunt for Major Finch began – or the *appearance* of the hunt, which was just as Holmes wanted.

I followed Holmes into the centre of the green, where he stopped. He pointed his cane several times in many directions, as if plotting out a waypoint, occasionally looking up in that direction before returning his eyes to scan the walls. As we came to the small stone wall we'd sat at earlier, he stopped and knelt. His eyes keenly scanned the grass, then he stood and wove a very odd path across that lawn to the old scaffold site, and directed me to a path that ran along past Beauchamp Tower, where he directed me to stop, and we found a bench under the cover of an old stone outer wall.

'We are safe to talk here,' Holmes said softly, lighting two cigarettes and handing me one.

'Aren't you concerned we'll be overheard? Would we not

be better in the open? Where long old stone-wall corridors can't carry our every word in multiple directions?'

'Excellent reasoning, my dear friend, but if you'll observe more closely, you'll see that this bench is in fact set within a heavy rock recessed wall, assuring us of almost silent conversation.'

Holmes was correct. I hadn't noticed how closed in we were. But as we spoke, it was clear the sound of our voices was being damped by the surrounding stone.

'Now you've observed our position further,' Holmes said, 'perhaps you'll also note why the choice to sit here was not done by chance?'

'Well, I *assumed* you picked this spot for a reason,' I offered, not fully cognisant *of* that reason. 'Although I am not sure—'

'Look up, what do you see?'

'An ancient old stone ceiling' – I paused as the realisation hit me – 'we're not visible from any position above us. Clever.'

'There are several locations that afford the protection of prying eyes, but only a few where a conversation might *not* be overheard – as you rightly pointed out before – and concealing the location of those having it.'

'I understand you didn't lead us here by chance, so what have you seen that I haven't?'

'Finch's footprints,' Holmes said smugly. 'I followed them this way – or rather, some of the way. I was careful enough to weave a path that did not follow them directly. If he was paying attention – which he was – Finch would have seen me on his track, but then leave it for an alternative to the one he laid out. It was a test of my intelligence,' he said. 'One I made sure to fail.'

'You know where he is, then?'

Holmes shook his head. 'Only where he was less than an hour ago.'

The surprise must have shown on my face, because Holmes chuckled. 'He crossed the lawn. Those footprints were not there earlier, or I would have seen them, so Finch made them when everyone was in the guard house – and he let us know it by stopping to smoke a cigarette at the very spot *you* were standing at earlier. Practically one pace behind you.' Holmes recovered a cigarette end from his pocket. 'He dropped this. A fairly common brand, unremarkable and untraceable, sadly.'

'Why would he put himself out in the open for all to see?'

'Ah,' Holmes said, slapping his knee. 'Because he's smart, Watson. I *always* suspected he could move around comfortably, because he's able to see where we are at all times, but *now* he's showing us he can actually move with impunity' – Holmes finished his cigarette and flicked it onto the grass – 'and right under our noses.'

'The brazenness of the fellow!' I retorted.

Holmes shrugged. 'And yet he is also a stimulating opponent to out-think. It really is an intellectual treat, Watson. Do not give me that disapproving face. I recognise it must sound terrible to you to hear me speak that way, but when I meet such a challenge, it invigorates me beyond the measure of anything else. Outwitting the perpetrators will certainly be a fair reward for our trouble, don't you think?'

I could not help but laugh. 'Although petty cash from the Crown might also aid us!'

'That also,' Holmes agreed.

'Well, where did he go then?'

My friend pulled out his map and pointed. 'Here. The old Chapel.'

'Should we not go there?'

Holmes shook his head. 'That would serve no purpose. He isn't likely to be there now.'

'What if he left the jewel there? Surely we should check?'

'Let us not concern ourselves with the jewel. It was simply a means to bring us all together. We will spend *our* energy on understanding the purpose behind *that*. Let the police concern themselves with missing stones.'

'You said earlier you intended to let Finch make his escape.'

'Yes,' Holmes acknowledged. 'This fellow, Finch, has a

first-rate intellect, but Finch *is* working with another, and they possibly have a larger agenda. It seems to me this person just might be even brighter. There is something familiar about the means behind my coercion.'

'Your coercion?'

Holmes chuckled. 'Oh yes. The subtlety of this drama is not lost on me. A stone is taken from her Majesty's keeping, and her Majesty calls for me personally. She then elects to speak with me, but hardly tells me anything of consequence. Really, Watson. The more I think about it, the more I suspect…'

'Suspect what?'

'Myself,' Holmes replied, with a smile. 'Of coming to conclusions too quickly.'

'I see. Well, I suppose it makes sense that you'd need to let one go to catch the other.'

Holmes beamed at me. 'To catch the real culprit,' he corrected.

'I'm glad to hear you say that,' I replied.

My friend nodded, then stood. 'I should like to make a quick review of the Bloody Tower.'

'You think we'll get a clue in there?' I asked, as I followed Holmes away from the bench.

'No,' my friend said, checking his pocket watch. 'We'll get nothing new for at least thirty minutes.'

That confused and surprised me. 'How can you know that?'

'Because I'm far better at recognising patterns than you are, it seems,' he said, patting my back.

'Apparently so.' I chuckled. 'So, what's the interest in the Bloody Tower?'

'Well,' Holmes said, leading me along the path. 'Legend has it was named after the supposed disappearance of the twelve-year-old Edward V and his younger brother, Richard. The story has it that the future King of England and his brother were both ensconced in the tower prior to Edward's coronation, but then the boys were declared illegitimate, and subsequently disappeared. Soon after their uncle, Richard III, ascended the throne.'

I chuckled. 'I see. A mystery in time, eh? I can see why you'd be interested.'

'Even I couldn't possibly solve a four-hundred-year-old mystery,' Holmes said with a laugh. 'But to see the place and imagine what *might* have occurred, well…'

It was rare for me to see Holmes excited about anything other than the case we were currently engaged upon, but I suppose even he – as unromantic and unsentimental as he often was – may have been influenced by the intrigue of the Tower of London, with its whimsical historical nostalgia. As a monument, of course, it is the silent stone witness to our darkest and most bloody times, the quiet spectator to a thousand terrible horrors, and those gruesome events – in details so grotesque – were now told to entertain the insatiable curiosity of large groups of eager school children, along with the public and other world travellers, as they enthusiastically gawp at the very instruments of those awful terrors. Holmes, of course, delighted in every aspect. For me, it was enough to make me pull my jacket just a little tighter to quash the chill it bestowed.

Chapter Five

'You're saying there's another person here we hadn't accounted for?'

The fine spring day soon gave in to a typically British afternoon of wet weather, which rather hampered the investigation. After our time at the Bloody Tower, Holmes checked his pocket watch and commanded us to return to the Jewel House, where he remained in review of those precious Crown artifacts for several long minutes. I stood by the window, looking down at the large view of the green and the guard house. I could see the stone wall we'd sat at, and the paths we'd walked during the day. It was possibly one of the better observation posts. I was just scanning the ground again when I noticed something disturb the ravens. For a moment, there appeared to be nothing, then a sudden movement caught in my peripheral vision. A fellow, dressed in something dark, possibly a long rain overcoat, shot out from somewhere to my left – just outside of my field of view – and darted across the lawn.

'Holmes!' I called, and in an instant my friend was beside me. 'Look.'

'Ah,' Holmes said, checking his pocket watch, the sparkle in his eyes ever present. 'Our confederate makes his move.

Excellent. It gives me new data to work from.'

'You were expecting this?'

'Or something like it,' Holmes acknowledged. 'This fellow is extraordinarily clever. He has a system of time that I haven't quite broken. The intervals are seemingly random, yet with each instance I hope to see a pattern.'

'There have been others?' I asked in a frown.

'Three,' Holmes said. 'Each time, as I said, at differing intervals. The first was ten minutes, the second fifty, and the third thirty.'

'Ten, fifty, and thirty,' I said in thought. 'It means nothing to me. I know how you like mathematics, but to me, those numbers do seem random.'

'Nothing is ever truly random, though,' Holmes remarked. 'There are patterns in everything. It's just another puzzle to solve.'

We observed the man reach a small walled area and appear to study it. The distance afforded us little detail, but fortunately Holmes was better prepared, choosing on that day to bring the cane with a small telescope inside the handle.

'Well,' he said, looking through the lens. 'It's impossible to see who it is. They've covered themselves well with that heavy rain coat – and with their back to us, I can see little through the downpour. Given his size, it's a constable or Warder.'

'What's he doing?'

'Right now, he appears to be relieving himself against the wall.'

'Oh bother,' I said. 'It's just one of our men, then?'

Holmes continued to scrutinise the fellow. 'It's impossible to know for certain,' he said. 'He's finished now. Let's see what he does next.'

There was a whistle from somewhere, which resulted in a rally of other whistles. We heard a shout from above, and then the sound of several pairs of boots clamouring along stone, where they emerged onto the lawn. Four men, two guards and two others, all in similar protective weather gear. They chased after the fellow, who simply waved at them.

'What's happening?' I asked.

'They're talking to the fellow,' Holmes said. 'Apparently, they've decided he's not a problem. Look, you see them waving to the men above?'

I took his place at the window and saw the group huddled in the rain, one of them vigorously waving a hankey. I then heard two sharp blasts of a whistle.

'The all clear,' Holmes said by way of explanation.

'A false alarm?'

'It might appear so,' Holmes said, taking my arm. 'Let us make certain.'

My friend led me down to the path, and we stayed under cover and free from the rain until it was impossible to do so. When we reached the path to the guard house, Holmes and I quickly entered and ran into the group of men, all removing their wet weather gear and hanging it near a large fire.

Holmes came amongst them to find the leader, who we discovered was a tall, thin sergeant. 'Where is the fellow you found outside?' he asked.

'Why, Mr Holmes,' the sergeant said. 'No doubt he'd be by the fire.'

Holmes growled at him. 'Five of you came in here, yet there are just four of you now. Do you see the fellow you met on the lawn?'

The sergeant called for attention, then quickly scanned everyone. He finally turned a red face to Holmes. 'He was in here, sir!'

'You three watch that door,' Holmes commanded. 'No one leaves.' He turned to the sergeant. 'Quickly man, where are the other exits?'

We followed the thin-faced Warder to the other exit and found the door wide open. The fellow had gone.

'I'm terribly sorry, sir,' the sergeant said. It was clear he was put out by it, and also angry.

'It wasn't your fault,' Holmes placated him. 'He was wearing the uniform of a police constable, was he not?'

'That's right. He said the inspector sent him down to do a

patrol, but it seemed odd, since we were on that route already.'

'You'd not seen him before?'

'Well, I'd not yet met all the policeman, sir,' he admitted. 'I recognised he was one, from his heavy police-issue raincoat. It just about covered him all up. I asked him for the phrase we were given and he gave the correct response to it. That's why I blew the all clear on my whistle, sir.'

Holmes nodded. 'Now he has apparently disappeared?'

'He could only have gone out this way, sir, or we'd have seen him.'

My friend stood in thought for a moment.

'Ought I to go after him, sir?'

Holmes shook his head. 'Would you go and explain this to the inspector? I'm confident it's all a simple misunderstanding. This fellow is probably with him as we speak – but best to be sure.'

'I'll do as you say. This fellow will probably come to regret he'd given *me* the run around,' the sergeant growled, and left us by the rear door.

As soon as the sergeant departed, I turned to my friend. 'You don't believe that, do you?' I asked.

'Not for a second,' Holmes replied. He then dropped to a knee and studied the wet prints. 'We have little time. Keep your eyes on that door,' he said, then followed those prints in a crouch to a wall cupboard and threw open the doors.

'The fellow took something out of here,' Holmes said, his lens now attached to his face as he ran it along every inch of each shelf. When he closed the doors, my friend gave a grunt of satisfaction. 'Interesting. Our confederate has helped himself to some supplies for his master,' he said, tapping the lens against his lips in thought.

'Such as?'

'One or two innocuous things. Shoelaces, cloth, cotton wadding, string, sewing materials, that sort of thing. Let's not get bogged down in the detail just yet,' Holmes replied. 'What's important is I believe these items were the reason our confederate came here.'

'So, it was his intention to come to this building?'

Holmes nodded. 'But why would he leave in so obvious a manner? It must attract the wrong attention, since...' Holmes took in a breath. 'Ha. Oh, Watson, this fellow is a genius.'

'What have you seen?'

'Seen?' Holmes grunted. 'Far too little. What's worse, I think we've been played.'

Several loud voices alerted us to the inspector and his men, who were clearly heading our way.

'Quick, Watson,' Holmes said, standing and throwing an arm towards the open rear door. 'The game's afoot once more, onwards!'

I followed him out into the rain, where we trailed those prints as they led from the guard house and into the muddy sides of various paths they interconnected with.

* * *

'What do you make of it?' I asked, as Holmes carefully examined the wall where we'd seen the confederate relieve himself earlier.

Holmes ran his gloved hands along every rock until he stopped and appeared to stiffen. 'Ah!' he said, and then he stepped back.

'What is it?'

Holmes shook his head. 'It's nothing,' he said, taking his cane from me. 'Let us get out of this rain and dry our overcoats.'

I admit the sound of that pleased me. 'Back to the guard house, then?'

'Yes. I need to have a quiet conversation with Gregson.'

I followed Holmes, who had his head bent forwards and cane resting on his shoulder, as he marched across the green towards the guard house. Inspector Gregson looked up as we entered.

'Just the pair,' he said, waiting until we'd discarded our overcoats and hats. 'There's fresh tea and coffee to warm you.

Or a nip of brandy, if you're wet to the bone as I am.'

We elected for coffee with a nip of brandy and stood warming ourselves by the fire.

'One of them Beefeater sergeants told you about the fellow they found on the green?'

'Yes,' Holmes answered. 'Watson and I observed him from Wakefield Tower, but by the time we arrived at the guard house, he was gone. He wasn't one of your men, then?'

'He wasn't,' Gregson said. 'Although he was apparently dressed as one.'

'That settles the matter,' Holmes remarked, smiling. 'Well, well. The ingenuity of our friend Finch knows no end.'

'You think it was him? Dressed like a constable?' I asked.

Holmes chuckled as he sipped his coffee. 'I sincerely doubt it. No, in my estimation, he's far too subtle for that. It's more likely he brought a friend back with him when he left earlier.'

The inspector's eyes widened. 'You're saying there's *another* person here we hadn't accounted for? And he's helping Finch?'

'I told you he was clever,' Holmes offered.

'So now I'm chasing two people around,' the inspector mused. 'I suppose it doubles our chances of catching them then.'

'Halves,' Holmes murmured into his cup.

I tapped his arm, and he chuckled.

'What was that, Mr Holmes?' Gregson asked.

'Oh nothing, Inspector. So, what is your next plan of action?'

The inspector grasped his lapels. 'The system appears to be working as set out. We'll continue to watch from above. Now we have two of them lurking about. It won't be long.'

'And where is Colonel Crowhurst?' Holmes asked.

'He's gone to the archives,' Gregson sniffed. 'The colonel said there are old plans of the early Tower build there. It's possible they'll help locate a secret passage or two.'

I turned to him. 'You don't seem that confident.'

The inspector shrugged. 'I'm not convinced such a robust prison would have that many, but I suppose it's better to be thorough.'

'I'm inclined to agree with you, Inspector,' Holmes said, although I couldn't be sure exactly what he was agreeing with. Gregson simply smiled.

'Do you have any more advice for me, Mr Holmes?' he asked.

'As it happens,' Holmes said, patting his shoulder. 'There are one or two things I should like to go over with you. I've written some suggestions in my book.' He reached into his left pocket and then his expression dropped. He checked his other pocket and sighed. 'Dear me, how annoying. In all the excitement earlier, I must have left my notepad on the table in Wakefield Tower. Watson, be a splendid fellow and go fetch it for me, would you?'

'Of course,' I said, nodding. 'I'll return as quicky as I can.'

'Thank you,' Holmes said. 'Oh, and Watson,' he said, taking my arm. 'No heroics, please.'

'When have I—?'

'It has been known,' he said, releasing my arm and turning back to Gregson.

* * *

I made my way out of the guard house into a downpour that had thankfully begun to diminish in strength, and hurried across the lawn to the tower's lower door and ascended the stairs up to the Jewel House.

It was the quiet that struck me first. I should have been challenged by the armed guard inside as I called out and opened the door, but I heard nothing. My long association with Sherlock Holmes had not endowed me with his intellectual gifts, it had to be admitted, but I had developed a rather healthy sense of danger, and so I cautiously peered around the door, slipping my revolver out of my jacket with practised ease, slowly cocking its hammer.

'Hello?'

Again, no response – and there should have been. A

challenge should come, one which I and very few others knew the correct response to. The heavy greyness outside had reduced the light within the room significantly. I could see from my vantage point the gas lamps, which I'd placed around the room earlier, were now extinguished. It left the chamber in far more shadow than I liked. Someone, I decided, had been there, and they'd either subdued or possibly killed the guard. I took a grip of my revolver and firmly pushed the door open enough to step into the room. Long shadows greeted me as my eyes attuned to the dimness. I scanned as much of the room as I could, hoping for a depth of detail other than just blackness, and was rewarded by some clear evidence that there had been a struggle. A table was upturned. Its chairs all strewn aside, and the papers that earlier sat atop it were now scattered across the old stone floor. My eyes now almost fully adjusted, I ventured further in, wincing at the sound my boots made on the stone floor – no matter how hard I tried, I could not make my tread light enough to lessen it. I continued my slow exploration, alert to almost every little sound. On reaching the upended table, I paused for a moment to scan the dark ahead. There were ample places one might conceal themselves and my mind had already begun playing tricks on me – turning every menacing shadow into Finch or his confederate – but on reflection it did appear as though the room *was* empty.

Where was the guard? I picked up Holmes's notebook and ran an eye over the papers. I pondered on Holmes's choice of words earlier. My friend often cautioned me against those heroic impulses. Sometimes, my sense of duty could pivot my thinking towards a tendency to rush in. I knew at this point it would have been wise to make a retreat and get him, and I was about to do so, when something caught my eye deeper into the room. My curiosity overrode that good sense and I stepped further in to investigate.

I stiffened a little and squinted. Jutting out of the darkness into a section of dim light just ahead of me, I thought I saw the sole of a boot. My first thought was, it might be the guard, and he might be hurt. I suppose my doctorly instincts took charge of my senses as I hastened towards him. At my approach, I was surprised to find a man lying prone. Although from my position I could not make out the features, I could tell it was *not* the guard – for he was not wearing a uniform. His silhouette also appeared far too bulky. I called out in a hush tone, to determine his conscious state. His lack of answer suggested he was unconscious which drove me forwards. I cautiously approached from the side and rather unexpectedly my legs gave way. My balance lost, I went headfirst down into a cold stone floor

* * *

Watson?... open your eyes!

I recall hearing muffled voices around me as I found my way back into the conscious world.

'He's coming around,' I heard someone say.

'I'll speak with the guard,' said another. 'See if he has answers for how this happened?'

The muffled and somewhat murmured voices sharpened as my eyes took in a face – my friend's face – whose rather concerned expression upon seeing my eyes flutter open quickly became relieved.

'Don't move, Watson,' Holmes said, checking my head. 'You were out cold for several minutes.'

'I'm hazy on details,' I answered, becoming more cognisant of my thoughts and surroundings. My head was pounding.

'How's your head?'

'Sore,' I admitted.

'How many fingers am I holding up?' he asked, and I chuckled.

'You don't have the tolerance to doctor me,' I replied. 'I'm fine, help me up.'

'Well, your sense of humour certainly appears unaffected.' Holmes seemed satisfied that I wasn't presenting symptoms of a concussion, and helped me to stand. I cast my eyes around the now brightly lit room and frowned.

'Where's the body?'

Holmes narrowed his eyes. 'Body?'

'Yes,' I said, pointing. 'It was here. I came beside it.'

Holmes came beside me. 'As you can see,' he said, 'there *isn't* a body.'

'Well, maybe the fellow was just hurt then. He must have left to get aid?'

Holmes took a greater interest in the floor. 'Gregson and I came looking after you took too long to return,' my friend said. 'When we arrived, the guard said—'

'But there *was* no guard, Holmes,' I hissed. 'The room was empty. Dark. That table…' My eyes caught sight of it. Someone had obviously righted it and neatly placed the chairs beside it. 'Well, someone had upended that table, Holmes, and they'd strewn your papers across the floor.'

Holmes rubbed his chin. 'Watson,' he said, lowering his voice. 'Aside from this oil-lamp, which leaked and appears to have caused your misadventure, this room was as we'd both left it previously. As you see it now.'

'That's impossible,' I growled.

'You're telling me the room was not in this state when you entered it?'

'I am,' I replied with as much confidence as I could. I found myself in conflict with my memory. I wondered if my recollections were the result of delusions from a concussion, however light it might be. Holmes, I was grateful to note, did *not* dismiss my rather confused recollections.

'I shall make a thorough examination of this room momentarily. You say the guard was not here when you arrived?'

'No,' I replied firmly.

Holmes flicked his eyes to the entrance door. 'Give me every detail,' my friend commanded me. 'Be as precise as you can be.'

I told my story as best as I could remember it. 'And that's *all* I recall. Say you believe me?'

'Despite your somewhat romantic susceptibilities,' Holmes

said, directing me to a chair, 'you may rely on two things from me. One, I will *always* believe you. Two, you will never have to ask *that* question of me again. Now, sit while I conduct my investigation.' He glanced over at Gregson. 'And say nothing about this to *anyone*. Agreed?'

I nodded.

Holmes then went about his work as Inspector Gregson came beside me.

'How are you feeling, Doctor?' the inspector asked.

'Fine, fine,' I said. 'Embarrassed.'

'Well, I, for one, am glad that you weren't seriously hurt.'

I frowned as a memory occurred that I had not detailed to Holmes. 'My revolver!' I blurted.

'Hmm, what was that? Revolver?'

'Yes, who has it?' I asked.

'No one has a revolver, Doctor. And I don't think it's wise for you to be carrying one either,' Gregson remarked sternly. 'You're sure you didn't hit your head harder than you thought?' His sympathetic look suggested his question was rhetorical.

I stood and smiled. 'Probably. Excuse me, would you?' Inspector Gregson nodded his head as I wandered away to where Holmes was staring down at the floor. I glanced back to see the inspector now speaking with the constable on the door.

'Watson,' Holmes said, somewhat crestfallen. 'I am sorry to report that I have so far found no solid corresponding evidence of your account, just circumstantial evidence. There are no drag marks suggesting a body was moved in or out. I found a smattering of footprints that could belong to anyone. It is rather perplexing. The fellow must have cleaned things up quickly.'

I raised my hand, and he frowned.

'Here's your evidence,' I said. 'Examine it and tell me what you see.'

My friend did as I instructed. He turned my hand over twice. 'A slight abrasion on the back made because of your fall. Reddening of the palm caused by something abrasive being rubbed forcefully against the skin. The lattice pattern appears symmetrical.' Holmes flashed me a grin, then raised my hand to his nose. 'As I suspected,' he said, dropping my hand. 'You were holding your revolver. The smell of gunpowder is strong enough to suggest—'

'I *fired* it as I fell,' I said. 'I'd forgotten that detail earlier. It just came to me.'

Holmes ran his convex glass along my hand and arm. He then brushed my sleeve with his hand and raised it to his nose. 'More traces of gunpowder. Interesting. We did not find you holding your revolver.'

'And I no longer have it.'

Holmes nodded. 'And since *I* have not found one in this room, we can now say with certainty someone else *was* here. Clearly, they took it.'

'The body?'

Holmes nodded. 'That seems the likely candidate, doesn't it?'

'Yes, but what does it mean?'

'There are several possibilities…' Holmes paused. 'You appear to have a theory of your own.'

I chuckled. 'Well, perhaps. It occurs to me that I may have stumbled upon Finch here.'

'Go on?'

'He heard me coming and shut off the lamps, and pretended to be unconscious, but the lamp he shut off near him leaked. I slipped in the oil and *he* took my revolver when I fell. He then put the room back as you found it and left me – possibly hoping that after hitting my head I'd not recall every detail. Will it do?'

To say Holmes looked impressed was an understatement. He nodded. 'Excellent, my dear fellow. It is a solid theory, but *one* thing doesn't fit. Why should he take your revolver?'

'That I can't answer,' I admitted. 'But disarming me can't hurt him.'

'True,' Holmes mused, lost in thought. 'But it goes against my idea of his intelligence. You see, if his idea was to make it appear your entire experience resulted from a concussion, keeping your revolver would seem to be an important aspect of that plan. Would you not agree?'

'I suppose so,' I said. 'But perhaps he took it for his own protection?'

'Perhaps,' Holmes said, then smiled at me.

'Just what was Finch doing here?' I asked. 'Why come back to the Jewel House, of all places?'

'One thing at a time,' my friend cautioned. 'There are several things happening at once, which we need to fit together. So far, we have events that don't appear to marry up.'

'I'd like to know where the guard was,' I said, looking to the military man at the door. 'What does he say about abandoning his post?'

'He says that he left briefly to relieve himself,' Holmes replied. 'That he'd locked the entrance door, and that he did not step into the room until we arrived to find you.'

'The door wasn't locked,' I said.

'That aspect clearly wasn't true,' my friend said, 'but it doesn't make his story a lie.'

'I wonder why no one heard my gunshot?'

Holmes shrugged. 'The various thick stone walls, along with that heavy downpour, dampened it sufficiently to a rumble we would all misidentify as a clap of thunder.'

'That makes sense,' I remarked, then added, 'except… Finch *couldn't* have assumed it wouldn't have drawn attention?'

'You are convinced it was Major Finch?'

'Who else could it have been?'

Holmes inclined his head and smiled at me. 'A good question. But to answer your first, whomever it was you interrupted *would* have expected it to draw attention – no matter how it might have sounded to us outside the room.'

'So, you'd already considered that then?'

'I had,' admitted Holmes.

'Could I have interrupted his plan?'

'It is possible,' Holmes offered.

'Finch must have put the room back after I fell, and left pretty quickly,' I said. 'Possibly *without* finding what it was he was looking for?'

My friend beamed. 'That bump on your head has done you good, Watson. Once again, you make a most excellent observation. I suspect we've turned a corner in our investigation.'

'You said earlier you needed Finch to make a mistake,' I reminded him.

Holmes just patted my arm and smiled at me.

Chapter Six

'He spends his time smoking that wretched pipe and doing little else.'

It was later that afternoon – when the grey clouds had dissipated, in their wake revealing patches of blue followed shortly by the rays of an afternoon sun – that I felt the oppressiveness of the day brighten and lift, like a great weight had been taken from me. The rain gave way to a fresh clean smell, which abated the irritation I felt at my earlier clumsiness. I stood on a wet lawn looking up at the White Tower and sighed. The case became more complex as time went on. We had not discovered Major Finch, or his confederate. We had equally not discovered the location of the King's Diamond, although I agreed with Holmes that in order for that to happen, we must allow Finch to reach it first – which meant keeping Gregson and everyone else away. Colonel Crowhurst had returned from his search of the archives, and brought with him old plans, which he and Gregson had poured over. Holmes had quietly directed me to where we stood now, and for a time he remained contemplative as he smoked his pipe.

'It'll start getting dark soon,' I mused.

Holmes said nothing, allowing great clouds to waft over his

head as he became further lost in his thoughts. I made a sideways glance at my friend, whose eyes were glazed and unfocused. He took another long pull on his pipe, then I saw those eyes focus and turn towards me.

'What is he waiting for?' Holmes finally asked me.

'Who, Finch?'

'Yes,' Holmes said, removing his pipe and emptying the ash. 'Why is he still trying to keep us all here? I must understand it.'

'The stone?' I suggested.

Holmes shook his head. 'I think it's apparent he could have collected that from any location by now.'

I rubbed my chin. 'I don't know the answer then. Do you?'

'There are several possibilities. We must determine first if my original suppositions were correct. There are some plausible reasons but the facts suggest that there are two possibilities. Finch can't leave, or he won't leave.'

'Both have different connotations,' I said in thought. 'If he can't leave, that might suggest whatever his business is at the Tower, he hasn't concluded it. You suggested earlier Finch concealed the jewel in some hiding place he hasn't been able to return to.'

'It's certainly in a place he cannot reach,' Holmes replied, nodding.

'But, if he *won't* leave… Well, I'm not sure what to make of that.'

Holmes smiled at me. 'It suggests a certain level of arrogance, doesn't it?'

'It does. It's almost as if Finch *wants* to be caught.'

'Perhaps,' Holmes said, chuckling. 'But the most likely answer is, there's something else going on that he either wants us away from, or wants someone else away from?'

I frowned. 'What do you mean?'

'We've failed to consider something vital in all this, but I think I am beginning to see the truth, if perhaps a little disjointedly.' He returned to filling his pipe.

'Such as?'

'I cannot say for certain. I rather suspect Sir Henry Ponsonby's accident plays some role in this. It cannot be a coincidence that after he is incapacitated, I am asked to investigate?'

My shock must have registered on my face, because Holmes gave me that knowing smile of his. 'Yes, Watson. As I said before. There is something else going on here.'

'Which of these events is the more important?'

My friend looked at me with an expression that appeared half surprised and half pleased. 'What an excellent question, my dear fellow. Which *is* the more important? The answer goes to the core of the case.'

'Surely the theft?' I pointed out.

'Why?'

I thought before answering. 'Well, because it *is* significant. I mean, the man entrusted with Her Majesty's jewels has himself taken it. Surely that warrants the biggest response.'

Holmes nodded. 'I wonder. Is it the act of theft that bothers you, or Major Finch's apparent betrayal?'

'Both,' I replied hotly.

'I see. And if the jewel had been removed by someone *other* than a member of the Queen's household,' Holmes persisted, 'would you feel as strongly?'

'Yes!' I blurted out.

Holmes raised his eyebrows slightly. 'Truthfully?'

My responses had been driven by my emotions along with a level of irritation and loyalty to Her Majesty; I knew that and so did Holmes. Sighing, I eventually shook my head. 'I suppose I wouldn't. The betrayal of Her Majesty upset me, I admit it.'

'Yes, and that betrayal has been the focus of all our motivations,' Holmes remarked, rubbing his chin. He appeared in deep thought. His eyes searching for something. 'It's become a personal thing,' he said to no one in particular. I observed his eyes narrow. 'In apparently stealing Her Majesty's diamond, Finch had ensured an emotional response from everyone… It's driven us all, Watson.' His eyes turned to me and they appeared startled. 'We've been *blind*.'

'What is it? What have you seen?'

'In order that we spared no effort in catching Major Finch, we have overlooked something. A subtle thing... And as I seize upon it, Her Majesty's request for help takes on an entirely different meaning.'

'I hope you intend to explain,' I said, not expecting anything of the kind.

'Yes,' he said. 'When the time is right.'

I sighed. 'Earlier you said you intended to let Finch go.'

'I certainly intended to do that,' Holmes replied. 'And as I come to a different view in this case. I must reflect on what I've seen and heard. I must better organise my thoughts, which will give me an opportunity to reorganise all the facts. Several instances in this case appear to have no connections, yet clearly they must. What troubles me, Watson, is how easily my thoughts and ideas have been subverted. It troubles me greatly.'

'Such as what?' My friend appeared lost. 'It's not like you to second-guess yourself,' I pointed out.

'This path of breadcrumbs hasn't led in a direction I expected it to. There are multiple overlaps in facts that make hardly any sense to me. Something is out of place, but for the life of me I cannot put my finger to it.' He appeared to decide. 'The answers must come after a period of inner reflection.'

'You intend to spend time in meditation?'

'I do,' my friend said. 'You've been invaluable, my dear fellow. I thank you.'

I wasn't entirely sure what I'd done to provoke my friend's gratitude, but was happy to accept a little praise from him.

'Go back to the guard house and wait there,' Holmes said, holding up his hand to forestall my inevitable argument. 'You've had an ordeal, Watson. The guard house is safe and warm with a cot you might take advantage of. I wish to be alone, and *you* need to rest.'

I knew it was useless to argue with him when his mind was so firmly set. Nodding, I followed my friend's instructions – inwardly pleased at the idea of a hot drink and a nap, and

Holmes being the observer of mankind clearly already knew it. I took my friend's advice and lay down for a time to assist my recovery, for although I hadn't admitted it publicly, I was fatigued and my head still pounded something terrible. I took a small dose of Chlorodyne and lay down for an hour while the potent mixture took effect. Although my headache had only subsided a little, I did not feel as though I wanted to spend the rest of the afternoon in that cot, so I got up and helped myself to a recently made pot of tea. I sat beside the window looking out at the dreary day, enjoying the brew, and thought about our strange case with its odd twists and turns. Holmes had reached a crisis, hence his need to deliberate – which I knew he'd explain in greater detail later. I couldn't help but wonder just what had caused him to consider something other than a jewel theft was occurring. I had seen nothing to indicate it, but then I knew Holmes's intuitions often went beyond what a normal person might perceive.

There was certainly a case to answer for Her Majesty's lost jewel and with it a case of mismanagement regarding how these things were controlled. Clearly, one man should not have sole access to the most expensive jewel collection in the world. If nothing else, the case highlighted a security breach of such magnitude that it must surely prompt a change in the way these things were managed. Most of Her Majesty's collection belonged to the country and was therefore essentially controlled by her government. I couldn't imagine that those "common men" would not order an immediate review of such practises for the future.

My recovery had almost completed by the time Colonel Crowhurst entered.

'Is there any news?' I asked.

'About Finch? No,' Crowhurst growled. 'I should like to have that devil locked up. There's no denying it. He's a danger to us all, and you should feel that danger better than anyone.'

'I should?' I asked, frowning at his suggestion.

'Indeed. Because of your earlier encounter.'

'As far as I know, I slipped on oil that had leaked from a

lamp, and hit my head,' I pointed out. 'I can't be sure of anything else beyond that.'

'Are you sure that Finch didn't attack you?' the colonel persisted. He seemed surprised by my reticence to affirm his suspicions. Had it not been for Holmes, who had shown me clear evidence of my accident, I *might* have agreed with him.

'I honestly can't recall,' I said, somewhat airily.

'I believe it was Finch, and there's an end to it. He's probably walking around with your revolver as we talk,' Crowhurst stated with a finality that surprised me. How could *he* be so sure when *I* couldn't be?

'I don't suppose anyone has found the jewel?' I asked, attempting to steer the conversation in a different direction.

Crowhurst ground his jaw as he shook his head. 'That too is in the wind, like a lot of things in this miserable business. Gregson has done little – although I suppose that was inevitable – and as for Mr Holmes?' He paused then sighed. 'I have to admit, I am a little disappointed.'

'How so?'

'Well,' Crowhurst grumbled. 'What has he done? Nothing. Has he offered any new suggestions? No. He spends his time smoking that wretched pipe and doing little else.'

I chuckled, which deepened the old fellow's frown. 'Holmes has his methods, Colonel,' I said, attempting to placate him. 'You *must* give him time.'

'Must I?' Crowhurst grunted, raising an eyebrow. 'And in the interim we're to do what? Sit around and wait? There's no point in hoping Gregson will solve things, although at least the man is out there attempting to earn his pay. Holmes is doing nothing.'

'Mr Holmes will always think things through first,' I said by explanation for the colonel's perceived lack of action. 'It might appear as though he's doing nothing, but I assure you he isn't. Action without a plan is a wasted effort,' I said. 'You should understand that.'

The colonel grunted again.

'Look, I don't always agree with his methods, but I trust

him, and apparently so does Her Majesty – and with respect, you should too.'

Colonel Crowhurst's hard, narrowed eyes softened. 'Of course,' he said. 'Forgive me, I'm just… well, I suppose I'm frustrated. I'm sure my observation of our detective friend's apparent inaction is entirely unjustified.' The colonel then lifted his chin. 'But we *do* only have his word that Major Finch remained here,' he pointed out.

I had to admit that the colonel was not wrong, but despite that, I defended my friend. 'I have no reason to doubt Mr Holmes,' I said.

'You might not,' Colonel Crowhurst said, 'but I don't know him as well as you.'

'Holmes was correct about the confederate,' I said pointedly. 'He'll be correct about everything else too, you mark my words.'

'I suppose you're right,' Crowhurst acknowledged. 'If Finch *is* still here, then why is this other fellow running around subverting and making us chase our tails?'

'I really don't have an answer for that,' I replied.

'I suppose we'll just have to wait for Sherlock Holmes to explain it then,' Colonel Crowhurst said. The look he gave me suggested he wasn't happy about it. Crowhurst sighed. 'I want this thing finished. I want the jewel back in *my* hand and Finch locked behind a set of iron bars.'

'Bringing our villain to justice,' Sherlock Holmes said as he entered the guard room via the rear door, 'is something we can *all* agree on.'

'Ah, Mr Holmes. Is there any news?' Crowhurst asked as we turned to greet him. I noticed the colonel's demeanour had changed slightly – evidently he did not wish for Holmes to see the frustrations he'd just alluded to; little did he know what subtle cues Holmes might have already noticed just from a brief look.

'None. Well, nothing that will please you,' Holmes replied, nodding to me.

'Your inaction hasn't pleased me all that much,' Crowhurst

grumbled. He rubbed his eyes. 'Why you'd think this would be any less annoying, I really cannot answer.'

My friend inclined his head. 'It is a troublesome business,' he remarked. 'I recognise waiting this fellow out must seem tiresome, but at this moment I believe it is the only thing we can do.'

'You're *sure* Finch is still here?' Crowhurst asked.

Holmes nodded. 'And to answer your next question, I am equally certain the stone is here too.'

'*How* are you certain?'

'For the reason I gave you before.'

'You don't have any proof of these claims, it's all just speculation on your part.'

Holmes nodded. 'You aren't entirely wrong. I ask you to trust me, Colonel, for just a little longer,' he said solemnly. 'The answers you seek will soon come.'

Crowhurst nodded. 'And in the meantime, you've Gregson and the military men moving around the place like a bunch of chess pieces,' he said. 'Don't think I missed that.'

My friend stood with his back to the fireplace. 'I don't deny it. It is my opinion that these fellows will serve us better if they are out of the way.'

'I see,' the old colonel said, 'which tells me you *have* a plan.'

'The early stages of one, certainly.'

Crowhurst appeared pleased. 'I should like to understand it.'

Holmes, however, shook his head. 'All in good time, Colonel,' he said. 'Watson will tell you, I only discuss a theory once I've tested enough of the links to make it solid. I am currently working on two and whilst they appear solid, they cannot work in tandem. That means one of them is incorrect.'

'I demand that you tell us,' Crowhurst growled dangerously. 'That way, *we* might help forge those links or at the very least help disprove one over the other?'

'When I am ready to share, you will be one of the first to hear it,' Holmes said. 'I'll tell you this much. Major Finch has played a very careful game. He has a plan, but it doesn't simply involve the diamond, there's something deeper and far more interesting developing alongside it,' he said, apparently studying Colonel Crowhurst for a reaction. If he expected the old soldier to appear startled, then he was disappointed.

'What nonsense is this?' Crowhurst asked.

'Finch is playing a long game, Colonel. And it might not be as we initially expected.'

This did get a reaction. I saw the old soldier swallow. It was a short, involuntary action, but it was enough to suggest that Holmes had hit upon something that Crowhurst understood. 'So, what are you saying now? Finch stole the jewel for reasons *other* than to make money from it?'

Holmes appeared pleased by either the colonel's reaction or his statement – or possibly both. 'Yes, that's *exactly* what I am saying.'

'And what makes you think that? It's not like a lot of things have changed since you caused him to run.'

Holmes inclined his head. 'I've had a moment to think,' he said. 'There were several key indicators of his motive visible earlier, although I admit I was slow to pick up on them.'

Again, Crowhurst seemed taken aback. 'What other purpose *could* he have then?'

'Let's just say I'm keeping an open mind on *all* motives. For now, I propose we allow things to proceed as they did before. No matter what Finch's plan is – however he intends to play it out – it must be allowed to proceed apparently unimpeded. He's a clever fellow, and he knows I am also. I therefore must continue to make errors, subtle enough that he doesn't suspect the ruse, but consequential enough to draw him into—'

'Making a mistake of his own?' I interrupted.

'Exactly so,' Holmes replied.

'I still say there is great danger in what you propose,' Crowhurst argued. 'Her Majesty—'

'Will weather the loss of a diamond with grace and dignity,' Holmes stated, crossing his arms. 'Please understand, Colonel, and I say this with the deepest of respect, I am not seeking your permission, nor do I need it. I have my methods and I shall do as I see fit to bring this entire affair to a satisfactory conclusion.'

Crowhurst appeared further annoyed. 'But to *whose* satisfaction, that's what I'd like to know.'

'Mine,' Holmes replied. 'For now, I'll let the police and the military men move around the board – as you suggested before – but *not* without purpose. Men of action, Colonel, feel better when they have something to do. So, I've given them something to do.'

'But you don't believe they will accomplish anything by doing it?'

'I didn't say that,' Holmes countered.

The colonel frowned. 'Are you capable of giving a straight answer to a question, Mr Holmes?'

'I am,' Holmes replied. 'When it suits me to do so.'

'Then tell me this. What is it you'd have *me* do?'

'Nothing.'

Colonel Crowhurst stared at him before answering. 'Nothing?'

'There's no need for you to do *anything*,' Holmes said. 'In fact, it would be helpful if you might consider heading home for the night. Should there be any news, I'll ensure you're one of the first to hear it.'

Colonel Crowhurst thought for a moment. 'Perhaps you're right. There *are* matters outside of this one I should attend.'

'Excellent,' Holmes said.

'I'll have a chat with the inspector first, then leave you to it.' And with that, the old soldier turned and walked away.

Chapter Seven

'A person's life now depends on us.'

I did not understand why, some twenty minutes later, Holmes had hidden us at one end of a wall while he peered around the stonework watching for something. My friend had been careful to ensure neither of us were seen heading in any particular direction. His grasp of the layout was so good, he led us quickly on a haphazard journey that by the time it concluded, and he'd settled us where we now stood, I could not immediately tell where we'd ended up. All I *could* tell for certain, from the overhang above us, was that we were certainly hidden from aerial view, meaning Holmes did not want anyone seeing us.

'Where are we, and what are we doing?' I hissed.

'We're watching the entrance,' Holmes muttered back.

'Why are we watching the entrance?'

'I wish to be certain Crowhurst has left us. Ah, yes, I see him,' Holmes said, extending the telescope handle of his cane, and looking through the eyepiece. 'He's boarding a carriage now. Splendid. Now that the good colonel has gone, we can move to the second stage of my plan. Come, Watson.'

I admit I was startled by this news. 'What second stage?' I

asked, as I attempted to keep up with him.

'No more questions,' Holmes said and pointed. 'This way,' he directed. I followed as he led us to the same seated recess we had been in before.

Now that we were alone and unlikely to be overheard, I turned to Holmes. 'I'm sure that I am stupid,' I said as we sat together on that familiar bench once again. 'But what did you mean by second stage?'

'Ah, well, stage one would be the removal of Crowhurst from the Tower.'

I frowned. 'And that was necessary because…?'

Holmes cocked his head a little. 'We'll never entice Finch out of hiding all the time the colonel is here.'

'How will he know Colonel Crowhurst has left?'

'His spy will know, and that suits my purposes.'

I stared at Holmes. 'Obviously you've seen more in this case than I have?'

'That you may rely on,' Holmes said. 'My dear fellow, we've all been blinded by this case. It wasn't until you were attacked that I recognised the dangers more thoroughly.'

'I wasn't attacked, Holmes,' I countered. 'I slipped in oil – it was *you* who made that clear to me.'

Holmes patted my hand. 'Forgive me, but at the moment I suggested it, I knew you were looking for answers. The mind can be impressionable after a traumatic experience, so I gave you an answer and offered evidence to cement that suggestion as an indisputable fact in your mind. I might write a paper on it, since in your case it worked so well.'

'You coerced me into believing something that wasn't true?'

'That is what I said, yes.'

'But why?'

Holmes sighed. 'Because you would not have given such a convincing account to Crowhurst, had I not. There is more. The fall did not render you unconscious as you believed.'

'Then, how?'

'You were hit from behind, after you fell.'

I frowned. 'I don't recall.'

'And yet the evidence was there for anyone to see,' Holmes pointed out. 'Fortunately, you confided your story to me first. Now, if you'd care to think a little harder, some of those facts might come through. I shall help by telling you categorically that you did not slip in oil or anything else. There was no trace of it on your clothes, Watson. If your recollection was correct, there really ought to have been – at least on your shoes?'

Now that he explained it, I saw the truth of it. 'I don't know why I didn't recognise that before.'

'You might blame me for that. The answer for how you fell is obvious. Someone kicked your feet out from beneath you. A cosh was used to hit you from behind – but not before you fired your revolver. It saved your life. I believe you saw the danger of your situation and attempted to protect yourself. I found it unlikely an experienced soldier would have fired his weapon accidentally. It was always more likely you used it to protect yourself.'

'I recall now,' I said, as my memories of the event flooded back. 'I had just reached the body when it moved. He kicked out my leg when I stepped back. Was it Finch who attacked me?'

Holmes shook his head. 'No, but you were meant to think he did.'

'Then who?'

Holmes considered me for a moment. 'Let me ask this. Would you have fired your revolver without aiming it at a target?'

'No,' I answered. 'I wouldn't have fired indiscriminately, and certainly *not* unless I felt I was in immediate danger.'

'Exactly. Close your eyes for a moment. Picture the scene as you walked in. You've spotted something on the floor, a foot. You step forwards. It's a body. It moves when you move closer. You're startled, you take a step backwards, and your feet are kicked from beneath you. You still have a hold of your revolver. Tell me, who are you aiming it at?'

The blur of images cleared and the face of my attacker

came into focus. 'It isn't anyone I recognise. Certainly not Finch.'

Holmes nodded. 'Perhaps you'll see now how perilous your situation was?'

'I'm beginning to,' I replied. 'But I don't understand any of it.'

Holmes sighed. 'I told you before, there are events occurring in tandem that don't appear to have a connection – yet they must. I believe I now understand something of it. The question is, what did you walk into?' he asked.

'Well, I can *hardly* answer that,' I retorted.

'I know,' Holmes replied, patting my arm. 'But I believe I can.' He calmly pulled a large black velvet bag from his inside jacket pocket and opened it. 'You walked in on an attempt, I believe, to retrieve this. It was your interruption, and the firing off of your revolver, which caused them to abandon their plan. Once you'd been dealt with, they hastily put the room back together and made their escape.'

'Is that…?'

'Yes,' Holmes said, handed the bag to me. 'It is the missing King's Diamond.'

I gawped in awe as I gingerly extracted the magnificent uncut pink diamond from the bag, whilst Holmes lit his pipe. It was impressive, being about half the size of a chicken egg.

'They were looking for it in the Jewel room?'

'One imagines they expected to find it inside the outer display case, since it was the most logical place to hide it – no one would conceivably think to look there, because who would be foolish enough to conceal it right next to the Crown Jewels?' Holmes said.

'And you found it when you examined the room after you discovered me?'

Holmes shook his head. 'I did not find it.'

'Then how?'

He smiled at me. 'It was given to me.'

'By whom?'

'We shall come to that.'

'You've had the King's Diamond the entire time?' I blurted.

Holmes gave me a stern look. 'If you could just shout that a little louder, Watson. I'm sure there are a few people in the quadrangle who didn't quite hear it,' he growled.

'I'm sorry,' I murmured. 'You took me by surprise.'

My friend shook his head. 'You understand now how I knew Major Finch could not leave?'

'Because you had what he wanted most?'

Holmes shook his head. 'He alone knew I had it.'

'He knew? What are you saying?' I stuttered. 'You're not making any sense.'

'I am making perfect sense,' Holmes countered. 'I have tried frequently to lay it out for you, but you appear either unwilling or unable to see the truth of it. Let me then spell it out for you. Despite everything we've been told, there never was a King's Diamond, do you understand now? That,' he said, retrieving the pink stone from me and turning it over before his eyes, 'is worthless.' Before I could make a comment – and I rather suspect to prove his point – Holmes dropped the bonny jewel onto the stone floor, where to my utter surprise, I saw it chip as it bounced. He dropped to a knee beside it and pointed. 'Look.'

'It's *not* a diamond,' I said. My astonishment must have looked comical.

Holmes lifted the sliver and passed it to me. 'Despite its beauty, it is simply, as I suggested earlier, a lump of rose quartz and nothing more.'

'But Her Majesty believed…'

'The Queen,' Holmes said, collecting the quartz and standing, 'is as much a part of this affair as Finch is.'

'You can't mean…' I stood aghast.

'Watson, do you imagine for a moment that the Queen's Jeweller might mistake quartz for diamond?'

'I suppose not,' I conceded.

'Then ask yourself, what reason would he have to lie to

her?'

'I suppose if he *knew* it wasn't a diamond, he'd have no reason – but there must have been another reason he'd want to steal it.'

'Think about it,' my friend urged me. 'We've just proven it is worthless. Why then would he want to steal something he knew – and we know – has no value at all?'

'I see your point.'

'We have been working under the premise that the Queen is told a valuable jewel belonging to the Crown has been recovered. One that is aptly named the King's Diamond. She has heard of it, but never seen it. It is a lost relic from a forgotten age, but knowing that it came from the recently opened tomb of her aunt, the possibility it *might* be genuine seems highly probable.'

'That's all reasonable,' I offered.

Holmes seemed pleased. 'Now, let us rework that premise and see it from a different perspective. What if none of it was true at all?'

'What, you mean the business with the aunt's tomb?'

Holmes nodded. 'Exactly. What if the King's Diamond had never been found? Do you see where that might take us?'

'Not really?' I replied honestly. 'I mean, we *know* something was found, since you have it.'

My friend had a light in his eyes. 'I was curious about the story from the beginning. Hardly any of it was verifiable and we only have Crowhurst's word that anyone had actually *seen* this jewel at all.'

'You mean Crowhurst wasn't truthful with us?'

'Colonel Crowhurst had every reason to want us to believe this story, and why wouldn't we?'

Holmes made a good point, although I admit I could not see where it was leading.

'While you are contemplating that, ask yourself why Finch didn't remove the stone *after* he and Crowhurst first locked it away?'

'That's a good point,' I remarked. 'He would have had a

full twelve hours to escape with it. So why would he stay and essentially wait to be caught?'

Holmes smiled. 'And what answer might we come up with to explain that?'

'I thought it was so no one would suspect the Queen's Jeweller of stealing her jewels,' I offered.

'I suspected him immediately,' Holmes pointed out. 'Even Gregson saw that no one else *could* have taken it.'

'So why did he take it?'

Holmes pointed his pipe at me. 'Ah, well, that is the interesting thing. The most likely answer is because he was ordered to, Watson.'

'By whom?'

'By Queen Victoria, of course,' Holmes said.

I gave an intake of breath. 'You're saying Finch *isn't* a traitor?'

Holmes nodded. 'We've already established Finch was the only person who could tell it wasn't a genuine diamond. So, why didn't he tell the Queen that the moment he saw it?'

'I don't know.'

'Because she already knew, Watson. It was *she* who set this charade up – or rather, someone counselled her to do so. Major Finch has been acting on her behalf. When I heard about the account of the aunt's tomb – which was an inexplicable thing – I wondered what might precipitate such an occurrence. Now, sometimes tombs are opened to inter other family members within. When I examined the records Crowhurst had so generously supplied, it appeared this Dowager Queen had *no* such relatives. You might recall my asking Crowhurst if there had been any royals who'd passed recently?'

I did recall that. 'Yes, he seemed taken aback by the question.'

'And as his answer confirmed my suspicions, it became apparent that there was simply no reason anyone *should* open it.'

'So, the story was a lie?'

'The story was false, yes,' Holmes replied. 'But not entirely.

If you'll recall, the Queen mentioned her grandfather's tomb had also been opened. I suspect that's where the story idea came from. Her Majesty told Finch, and he came up with the rest.'

'But why!'

'Because Her Majesty is worried about something far greater than a trinket,' Holmes said. 'Do you honestly imagine she would call for my help for something as trivial as a lost diamond?'

'Well, the circumstances would have to be correct to pique your curiosity,' I said.

'Such as a diamond stolen from the Crown's collection held in the secure Tower of London, you mean?'

'Exactly.'

'I admit, I thought that was an excellent touch.'

I frowned. 'Did Crowhurst set this whole stolen jewel business up then?'

'No. Finch and Her Majesty orchestrated that ruse.'

'And they did it to gain your service?'

'As I see it, yes.'

'Well, why didn't the Queen just call for you directly? Why didn't she ask you outright to help her with whatever it is she really wanted from you? Why all this... theatre?'

Holmes laughed. 'Valid questions. The answers are, of course, elementary. Her Majesty is *never* alone, Watson. Even in private discussions with her government ministers, or at dinner with close family members, there are *always* courtiers and servants and guards in proximity. That goes to the heart of *why* she may want our help.'

'Agreed. So, what are we dealing with, then?'

'It is a delicate situation that she clearly feels some personal danger from. The cause of her concern was great enough to create this entire affair just – as you rightly pointed out – to engage my interest. If she had evidence that could be put before someone other than me, she'd have done so already. So, she only had those concerns.'

'Yet even when she was alone with us, she clearly felt

unable to speak of it,' I mused.

Holmes nodded. 'Suggesting that the perceived danger she felt was tangible – and present.'

I gasped. 'Meaning Crowhurst?'

'I fear so,' my friend said. 'It might also explain why Her Majesty went to such lengths to make it public knowledge that it was her intention to engage me. It was a message. I could not decide initially for whom. But it seems probable it *was* for Crowhurst, or perhaps for someone he is connected to, although I am convinced there were others. With Sir Henry out of the way, Colonel Crowhurst could maintain a position of trust that bore little scrutiny from anyone other than, say, the Prime Minister.'

'And you think the message was for him?'

'That I cannot be sure of. One thing is clear. Crowhurst was there when the Queen met us. Since she felt unable to speak of her concerns, well…'

I nodded. 'I would not have thought that old soldier could be so villainous.'

'We still don't fully understand his role in all this,' Holmes cautioned.

'Even so,' I said. 'He's guilty by association, isn't he?'

Holmes shrugged. 'We shall see.'

'So, who gave you the stone?'

'Her Majesty did,' Holmes replied. 'She clasped it into my hands right before she left us.'

Chapter Eight

'We have a long and dangerous night's work ahead of us.'

The revelation that Her Majesty the Queen had actually handed Holmes the stone before we even began investigating caused me to chuckle. I remembered the Queen taking Holmes's hand in both of hers, but it did not occur to me she'd done so to place the stone there.

'Good lord. But that means you've been feeding me numerous fictions all along. For what purpose? And does Gregson know any of this?'

Holmes slipped the fake King's Diamond into his pocket. 'The purpose should be rather obvious – to ensure that the right people are kept in the dark, I have kept *everyone* in the dark. As for Gregson, he understands *some* aspects of my suspicions. But until we know fully who these conspirators are, we must remain cautious. When I sent you to fetch my book, I detailed those concerns to him.'

I recalled he'd sent me to collect that book, and I also remember flicking through it briefly before my accident, and finding it practically empty. 'Yes, I wanted to mention that. As far as I could tell, your book contained no written suggestions that might have assisted Gregson with the case.'

Holmes gave me a thin smile. 'Ah. Yes, I apologise for that. The ruse was necessary. You see, in order to validate my suspicions, I needed a genuine excuse for you to be alone. I felt sure it would draw out those conspirators.'

My agitation grew. 'You *deliberately* put me in danger to prove a theory?'

'I'm sure it must appear that way,' Holmes replied calmly. 'I genuinely believed you would come to no harm.'

'Coshed over the head and left for dead!' I growled. 'I hope it was worth it?'

'It was,' Holmes remarked unemotionally. 'I suppose my methods brought about an unintentional salubrious effect for you, but I *could* prove my theory, and because of that, we *are* a lot further forwards.'

'Oh, so I should be thankful?' I rubbed at my eyes. It wasn't the first time Holmes had treated me this way, and I doubted it would be the last. 'How could you know Finch and his cohort would be there? The place is guarded at all times. Wait…' I frowned. 'There *was* no guard when I arrived.' Sudden realisation hit me. '*You* had the guard removed?'

'Of course,' Holmes replied in his nonchalant way that I found infuriating. 'The room needed to be accessible.'

'This is beyond anything I would have expected from you, Holmes,' I complained.

My friend pointed at me. 'And yet I distinctly remember telling you *not* to be heroic. I made the point strenuously, as I recall. At the first sign of trouble, you should have reported back. I admit and apologise that my actions put you in *some* danger, Watson, but please… it was *you* who walked knowingly headfirst into that danger.'

I shook my head at him. Despite our long association, his dispassionate logic could still surprise and alarm me. 'Semantics.'

'Facts,' he countered.

'I don't know what to say to you at this moment,' I grumbled, crossing my arms.

'You can be angry later.' Holmes's reprimand did little to decrease my irritation. 'For now, we have far more important matters to attend to. A person's *life* now depends on us.'

This statement caused my annoyance to lessen. 'Someone is in danger?'

'Several people are,' Holmes replied, nodding. 'And if I am correct, we have just under twenty-four hours to ensure they survive.'

'Who are these people?'

'Members of Her Majesty's household,' Holmes said. 'Possibly even Her Majesty.'

'Good lord!'

'Exactly,' Holmes said. 'I need data, and that is why luring Finch from hiding is necessary.'

A thought came to me. 'Are we to believe that Crowhurst is behind it all?'

'Colonel Crowhurst is playing a part,' my friend remarked. 'I think he understands a little of what I've uncovered, although he hasn't seen it fully. I've been careful to appear lacklustre.'

'Yes, he was complaining about that.'

'I am very pleased to hear it,' Holmes remarked. 'Crowhurst isn't that intelligent, but he *is* cunning. He's also dangerous, as you have first-hand experience of.'

'You mean it was Crowhurst who coshed me?'

'He was the one person we have named as a player in this affair, and the one person who was absent when you went to the Jewel House.'

'How can you be so sure?' I asked.

'He rather gave that away earlier, when you were talking about it.'

I frowned. 'I don't recall what.'

'I was stood by that rear door for a little longer than you both realised. He questioned you over the attack. As I recall, he tried to convince you it was Finch who had perpetrated it.'

I wasn't sure what Holmes was attempting to say. 'I didn't agree with it.'

'Rightly so. Crowhurst then said it was probably Finch who had taken your revolver.'

'That's true,' I nodded.

My friend chuckled. 'But how could he know that? You told me – and I forbade you from telling anyone else, which I believe you stuck to.'

I gasped. 'I did!'

'So, he could only know it if—'

'If *he* had taken it,' I cried.

'And if he took it, then it was he who coshed you. Et voilà!'

'The scoundrel.'

'Indeed,' Holmes said. 'Now, in order for us to move forwards, it is imperative Crowhurst should be absent.'

'Is Crowhurst working alone?'

'No,' Holmes said emphatically. 'Now, if I've gambled correctly—'

'Gambled?' I growled.

'If I am correct,' Holmes continued, ignoring my interruption. 'Major Finch has been doing his level best to *ensure* Crowhurst does not leave.'

'Why?'

'I only have a theory to answer it, and not a solid one. There are still pieces of this puzzle that don't fit together,' Holmes replied. 'But now *I've* persuaded the colonel to leave. My hope is it will draw Finch from hiding in short order, and then we may get the missing pieces of our puzzle from him. I suspect it won't be long before we understand the depth of this thing properly. I fear something dreadful is in the works.' Holmes then took my arm. 'Are you with me, Watson?'

'Well, of course I am,' I replied, shaking away the agitation.

My friend winked at me, then gave me a hearty pat on the back. 'Then let us channel any annoyances we have into solving this case.'

I gave him my best smile.

'We have a long and dangerous night's work ahead of us,' my friend said. 'Let us see if we can get the advantage.'

Sherlock Holmes checked his pocket watch a second time,

then looked up as a heavy cloud covered the descending late afternoon sun. Time was moving on and the afternoon light, such as it was, had already begun its transition to that mix of wintery-early-spring evening grey. Holmes stood under a sheltered section of outer wall, looking out as the rain shifted to a light drizzle. The weather made our afternoon wait seem much longer than it should have. Holmes smoked for several minutes, while I sat huddled in that chill. We'd been at the Tower of London since early morning, and I'd seen our case turned on its head as the day went on. Now, as damp permeated through my heavy tweed rendering me likely to catch a cold, I silently wished for the warmth of our fire and my comfortable slippers. I stood to warm myself. As I came beside Holmes, he turned and smiled at me. Evidently, the terrible murk and dampness had not affected him in the slightest.

'Anything,' I asked, possibly for the fourth time.

My friend shook his head, then took his pipe from his mouth. 'This location should give him adequate cover,' he said. 'I chose it specifically for that reason. Why hasn't the major come? He *must* come.'

'Is there no way to get a message to him?'

'We *could* go to his location,' Holmes said somewhat reluctantly. 'But I'd rather not give his position away. Since we know the Queen considered herself in danger, that must go double for Finch.'

I raised an eyebrow. 'You *know* where he's hiding?'

'Yes,' Holmes said, and nodded, apparently missing my annoyance at having been kept in the dark – again. 'There's a passage that leads from the back of the chapel to some old abandoned rooms in the building next to it. It's in a central location, essentially making it the best sentry point. He can come from the chapel, or use the passageway that goes beneath the green and ascends up to the Bloody Tower.'

'So that was the real reason you wanted to visit that tower, eh?'

'It was. When I studied the maps, there was a faint line that seemed to link to that old tower. Everyone was so involved with discovering secret tunnels and so forth, they really didn't consider those more strategic locations that were open and obvious. I said before Finch could come and go as he pleased, and when I saw that faint line on the map, which could easily have been a printing error – I made a brief inspection of the old tower room and discovered footprints leading out that were freshly made.'

'I didn't notice them,' I said.

'Nevertheless. Now Finch has been keeping an odd measurement of time to make certain his movements could not be easily predicted. I suspect Crowhurst has also been attempting to determine how he is making that distinction. There are several mathematical formulae that might explain it, but I feel sure it is something simple. I think I'll just make a quick survey of the wall Finch's comrade stood at earlier.'

'Why?'

'Well, it *is* an excellent location to leave a message.'

Realisation hit me. 'Of course. That fellow we saw earlier was leaving Finch a message and only pretended to relieve himself for anyone who was watching.'

'Exactly so.' Holmes took out his notebook, scribbled on a page, and tore it out. He then folded it tightly. 'Stay here,' he said, and in an instant he'd shot across the lawn towards the wall, which fell just outside the field of my vision since the dimming light had plunged it into a murky darkness. I squinted and just made out my friend as he stood at that wall, then saw him emerge as he dashed back and joined me.

'Now we wait,' Holmes said.

'Not for long,' I hissed, pointing. 'Look.'

'Oh, good eye, Watson!' Holmes said as he pulled me further into the shadows. We watched as a silhouetted figure appeared by the wall, then disappeared back into the murk. 'Excellent. Now we're getting somewhere. Let's head to the Bloody Tower.'

'That's where you told Finch to meet us?'

'I thought it wise to show my hand,' Holmes said. 'It's the

location he's been using to come and go all day. By asking to meet here, it should prove he can trust us, since my knowledge demonstrates I could have exposed him.'

'Let's hope you're right,' I said.

'Come on.' My friend led us back to that tower and I stood and was grateful to be out of the damp. I went to light the candle we'd used earlier but my friend stopped me.

'No,' Holmes said. 'Despite being enclosed, that candle might attract unwanted attention via the window.'

If anyone is even watching, I thought. 'You want us to wait in the dark?'

'If I am correct, we'll not have long to wait. A few minutes only,' my friend said.

I sighed as I pulled my collar up. Holmes stood with his hands planted firmly on his cane in the middle of the chamber, and I stood some distance to the side holding my heavy stick – wishing my revolver was still in my possession.

It was difficult to say how much time had passed before we heard a soft click, followed by a scraping from the wall ahead. To my astonishment, a large picture creaked open, and a hand holding a candle poked through to light the area. Finch then beckoned us inside, and both of us darted towards the picture and followed him onto an old stone staircase. The beardless Major Finch gestured for us to maintain silence as he closed the secret door, and we followed him down and into a long corridor, all the time saying nothing, and eventually we arrived at another stone stair, which spiralled up to a solid wall. Finch found an invisible handle and opened a panel that led us into the room he'd clearly been hiding in. After we'd stepped through, he closed the door, then placed his candle on a small table and gestured for us to sit. I looked up at the windows set into the stone above, but saw only the dark silhouette of a part of the Tower in the distance. I took the offered chair, but Holmes remained standing.

'Brandy?' was the first audible thing he said. Without waiting for an answer, he took three glasses from a cabinet, placed them on the table, and filled each with a generous amount of the liquid, collecting one and swallowing a good slug. It seemed to settle him.

Both Holmes and I took a glass and also drank.

'Where is your companion?' Holmes asked.

'You've ruined *everything*,' Finch grumbled with a sigh. 'Months of work. Now all for nothing.'

Holmes smiled. 'Because I coerced Crowhurst to leave?'

Finch nodded, then sighed. 'My companion. My trusted friend left to follow Crowhurst.'

Holmes nodded. 'Good. That is what I had hoped for. He will report back when?'

Finch pulled out a crumpled piece of paper and ran an eye over it. 'In an hour.'

'Then we have time to talk. Incidentally,' Holmes said, 'the frequency of intervals in time you've been using has me intrigued. They appear random, but I suspect you have a formula?'

Finch chuckled. 'Nothing complex, I assure you.'

I saw Holmes narrow his eyes in that way he often did when his brain was attempting to solve a puzzle. He finally grunted. 'I have it, you're using a six-sided die?'

Finch pulled a little bag and smiled. 'It seemed appropriate. I rolled it earlier and wrote each interval down. That way, I leave nothing to chance.'

'You're a clever fellow,' Holmes said. 'I have enjoyed my time attempting to decipher the full extent of this case, but now we must get to business. Had you been a little more open,' he said, dropping the stone onto the table. 'I *might* have been in a better position to aid you earlier.'

'I couldn't take the risk you weren't part of it. Her Majesty appeared to trust you, but that didn't mean you hadn't pulled the wool over her eyes. She doesn't always see the truth of things.'

My friend smiled. 'This conspiracy, you mean?' he asked.

Finch nodded. 'They're everywhere,' he murmured. '*Everywhere.*'

'And do *they* have a name?' Holmes asked.

'Not that I am aware of. It's a small group, but they're set upon harming our country through our Queen.'

I looked at Holmes and noticed his eyes scrutinising Finch. 'I see. I know you and the Queen set this charade up so she might coerce my involvement,' he said.

Major Finch nodded.

Holmes continued. 'And my conversation with Her Majesty indicated she thought herself to be in some danger, but could not, or would not, explain it. It suggested she did not want someone to overhear her, and I quickly concluded that to be Colonel Crowhurst—'

'Crowhurst is a lackey,' Finch blurted. 'Nothing more than a hired thug.' He quickly finished his brandy.

Holmes narrowed his eyes. 'Can you name other members of this conspiracy?'

'The Home Secretary for one,' Finch said.

Holmes rubbed his chin in thought. 'I see. Who else?'

'The captain of the Tower Guard,' Finch said, refilling his glass and shakily taking another large gulp.

I stood and collected the bottle, lest he should drink too much and rob us of any coherent answers. 'Let's go a little easy on that,' I suggested, putting the bottle out of his reach.

Finch gave me a look. 'Fair enough.'

'What is it you suspect these men of orchestrating?' Holmes asked.

'They have a design to replace the Queen,' Finch said.

Holmes frowned. 'Replace her? You have proof that will validate that?'

Finch stared at him. 'Possibly. It started out as a whispered conversation here, an overheard comment or two there. Nothing substantial.'

Holmes rubbed his chin. 'Forgive me, but that claim cannot be made without something to back it up. You say you have nothing?'

Finch nodded.

My friend studied him for a moment. 'Major Finch, it must

be apparent to you by now that I could easily have exposed you.' He leant forwards. 'You *must* trust me. It is the only way we might bring this entire affair to a close.' And just as he had done to Finch earlier, my friend held out his hand. 'If you want my help, you'll entrust all documents you have to me.'

Finch appeared to weigh up his options. He then looked between us and eventually gave Holmes a tight smile. 'Very well, Mr Holmes. I'll hand my evidence over,' he said, 'but only *after* I've told my story.'

Holmes nodded, taking a cigarette out of his box and lighting it. 'Go on.'

Finch gave a sigh. 'I suppose it started several months ago when Her Majesty explained someone might have taken a shot at her in the grounds of Buckingham Palace.'

Chapter Nine

'What was it that drew your attention to this danger?'

Holmes raised an eyebrow. 'Was an investigation made over her claim?'

'Yes. Sir Henry asked Crowhurst to lead it. However, it was deemed to have been nothing more than a mistake made by a guest, who was apparently inexperienced in shooting. The Queen put the entire affair behind her.'

'These things happen,' I offered.

'And what occurred after this incident to make you consider Her Majesty might be in further danger?'

'It started with a note—'

'Ah!' Holmes said. 'Now we get to it. A note, you say?'

'Yes. Apparently, Her Majesty had received several of them. They usually came the day before a planned event in her diary.'

Holmes smiled. 'Ingenious. They could hardly cancel those engagements at such short notice. Go on, Major.'

'Well, each time the note gave some warning that she should not attend, but apparently Her Majesty simply ignored them.'

'Until something occurred to make her consider these warnings?'

Finch nodded. 'A few incidents caused her to question things, it's true.'

'Such as,' I asked.

'Well, there was a fire in a warehouse that apparently started just after Her Majesty had toured it. She left before anyone noticed it. I understand several people *were* killed.'

Holmes rubbed his chin in thought. 'A coincidence.'

'Possibly, but then a week later the floor gave way in St Mary's hospital killing eight of the medical staff, and wounding around twenty others. Was that also a coincidence?'

'I recall that,' I remarked, turning to Holmes. 'You made a review of it, if I am correct?'

'I did,' Holmes said. 'My conclusions did not indicate foul play. You are saying the Queen received a warning the day before this event?'

'She did,' Finch said. 'And she toured *that* floor just six hours before it fell away.'

'Interesting,' mused Holmes, 'and suggestive.'

Finch finished his brandy. 'The warning held no details – they didn't say what would happen, only that something might, you understand? They contained dates, times, and a scribbled warning.'

'And how did these warnings reach Her Majesty?'

'The notes were written on House of Common's letterhead, and came in her dispatch box.'

'Ingenious,' Holmes said. 'Guaranteeing they'd always be seen by Her Majesty first.'

'They were right at the top too,' Finch added.

'And as those boxes are delivered once a day from various government departments, via the Page of Presence,' Holmes detailed, finishing his cigarette, 'there's no way anyone could tell from which department those notes might originate from.'

'You have it right,' Finch replied. 'And once they arrive at the palace, only her Majesty's key can open those boxes.'

'Someone in government was sending these warnings,'

Holmes mused for a moment. 'And you haven't discovered who?'

Finch shook his head.

'How did you become a part of this?' I asked.

'Through Her Majesty. We meet twice a week. One evening,' Major Finch said, leaning forwards, 'we were discussing a jewelled brooch which she had designs to purchase for a relative. Her Majesty often worked as we talked, and so it wasn't unusual for her to open her box for something. Well, when she gasped, I looked up and saw how startled she looked. Without preamble, she angrily thrust a paper into my hand. I've always enjoyed a slightly personal relationship with Her Majesty, and maybe that's why she allowed me to see this document. As soon as I read it, I recognised what it was. A warning. She then told me it was the *fifth* one she'd received. On each occasion one had arrived, some calamitous situation occurred at the very event it referred to.'

'Had she raised her concern to anyone?'

Finch nodded. 'Her Majesty told me she intended to take the matter up with the Prime Minister – but I understand he was abroad – so the Home Secretary came in his place. During their interview, Her Majesty said he seemed interested in them, but told her to pay them no attention. As far as I understand it, she never received another after that.'

'Do you still have these notes?'

Major Finch gave a slow nod.

Holmes smiled. 'If Her Majesty no longer received any, after speaking with the Home Secretary, then either the writer was alerted and stopped his warnings, or the monarch's dispatch boxes were further scrutinised after packing, and someone removed any new notes prior to those boxes being dispatched.'

'I believe the former, but I suppose the latter could also be true. All I know is Her Majesty was happy the situation appeared resolved. But I wasn't convinced,' the major stated. 'Her Majesty could never openly question or investigate such things, but I could, so I called in a favour from a friend.'

Finch lifted his glass and waved it at me. I looked to Holmes, who nodded, and so I opened the bottle and poured a little into his glass. He seemed grateful.

'Captain Harold Green was a member of my old regiment,' he began. 'He was a first-rate soldier, but after a brutal month of fighting on our last tour in Afghanistan, he told me he intended to end his service when his tour was complete. True to his word, he did just that. He found himself back in civilian life and not long after he got himself elected as a member of Parliament, and was offered a decent job at the Home Office. I approached Harry and told him everything I knew. He said he'd make some enquiries, and it wasn't long afterwards that I recognised I'd put myself and my friend in danger.'

'What was it that drew your attention to this danger?' Holmes asked.

'A few rough-looking fellows began hanging around my house. They looked out of place. The next day they were there again, and the day after. It occurred to me someone was now watching *me*. Could it have been whoever had been causing these terrible incidents? Might they now have set their sights on me?'

Holmes extinguished his cigarette. 'You didn't suspect it could have been the person sending the warnings?'

Finch shook his head. 'I didn't. These men were sinister looking. Anyone who might take the time to warn of some potential harm, I suspect, would look less foul. Anyway, my suspicions were confirmed when Harry came to me. He told me pointedly that I'd got myself and him mixed up in a dangerous business. He wouldn't tell me anything more, Mr Holmes, but I saw he was scared, and I'd *never* seen him scared before. Harry warned me against asking questions, and I took that warning seriously. He told me he was looking into something. It went pretty deep. Harry came across some startling evidence involving senior members of government, but again he wouldn't go into detail.'

Major Finch rubbed his eyes. 'Harry telegraphed me two

days after and asked me to meet him at our usual spot. It was a café in Westminster. He never arrived.' Finch looked terribly sad. 'I heard they'd found him dead outside Westminster station that morning. A thief had repeatedly stabbed him – so the police told me. The thing is, Harry was a first-rate soldier. A proper fighter. He taught hand-to-hand defence in the regiment. I find it very hard to believe *anyone* could have killed him the way they said. The police told me he didn't appear to have put up a fight. I didn't believe a word of it. I once saw Harry take on three mean Afghans armed with knives, and all he had was a stick. He didn't even break a sweat sending them on their way.'

'You viewed the body?' Holmes asked.

'They wouldn't allow me to,' Finch said. 'Family only, but Harry had none.'

Holmes was thoughtful. 'You believe someone in government ordered his murder?'

Finch nodded. 'And I think whoever did it was no street thief, either. After that, I played things pretty tight to my chest in case I did something that might warrant them murdering me too.'

'Wise. You spoke with Her Majesty about it?'

'Not initially. I kept it to myself, but soon after I received a letter in the post. Harry must have sent it the day he died. It contained a bunch of papers he'd put together. It was thorough, Mr Holmes. Accounting records showing large funds being moved to businesses. Everything linked back to the Home Secretary. There were communication logs between various people; honestly, I couldn't make much sense of it. It's all there,' he said. 'When I realised Harry might have been killed for discovering it, and that it might go badly for me if the wrong people found out I had all that stuff, I confided my fears to Her Majesty. But the Queen isn't equipped to deal with things of that nature, and I shouldn't have burdened her. Sadly, her instinct was to put it all before Colonel Crowhurst.'

Holmes appeared to understand his misery. 'And after that, the target was set square on you?'

'Regrettably,' Finch moaned. 'I had one thing in my favour. They didn't know I had all those papers.'

'When did you discover Crowhurst was a part of this conspiracy?' Holmes asked.

'First, I never fully trusted the man. Harry told me Crowhurst had gained his rank through backdoor promotions. There are many rumours about him. One suggests his father, Captain Crowhurst, was a merchant in India who helped a wealthy maharaja wanted by the British to escape. He was handsomely rewarded for doing so, but a member of Crowhurst senior's staff turned him in to the local governor and Crowhurst senior was tried and subsequently executed.'

'British justice in India is swift,' I said.

Finch nodded. 'Colonel Crowhurst was a young man who'd only recently been commissioned when it happened. The way Harry told it, Crowhurst escaped with the aid of his father's treasure and made it to England, where he climbed the ranks by using that wealth.'

Holmes frowned. 'You believe Crowhurst might wish to cause harm to the monarch because of what happened to his father?'

Finch nodded. 'He got himself all the way to the Queen's private secretary, didn't he?' Finch said.

'Temporarily, at least.'

'Before that, he was part of Her Majesty's personal entourage,' Finch added.

'If what you say is true, then this vengeful man appears a patient one,' Holmes mused. 'Having made his way up the ranks to get within striking distance of the Queen, he then pauses before enacting this revenge for his father's death,' Holmes said, giving him a look. 'Why did he wait?'

Major Finch shrugged. 'I didn't say I had *all* the answers. One thing is clear to me, though. He couldn't do anything while Sir Henry stood between them.'

'Ah, so you believe Sir Henry's accident was nothing of the kind?' Holmes asked.

'It all seemed a bit convenient, don't you think?'

Holmes nodded, but said nothing.

Finch continued. 'And once Crowhurst was in power, things changed. I felt there was imminent danger to Her Majesty because of it – not that she initially saw it. Keeping Crowhurst here at the Tower was my only plan, since I *knew* he couldn't harm Her Majesty as she was on her way to Osborne House.'

'Your little charade with this,' he said, lifting the stone, 'was twofold. To pique my curiosity and gain my service, and to sway the colonel, who clearly believed your ruse over the origin of this fictitious King's Diamond. A story so full of holes, I'm surprised the colonel didn't see through it.'

Finch smiled. 'All I had to do was say it was real. The rest was easy enough, since he'd have no reason to question it. I had to think hard about how I was going to keep him here. Then you arrived and immediately outed me,' Finch said, smiling.

'Having read something of the situation, it seemed the appropriate thing to do,' Holmes replied.

'And it all worked beautifully after that. I knew Crowhurst suspected me of stealing the jewel, but I think he also discovered my friendship with Harry too. He had a way of letting you know he knew things. Things he ought not to know. But despite what he might have had on me, I believe my closeness with Her Majesty was a bigger asset for him. I used it to stay ahead of any potential retribution.'

'Which was an intelligent thing to do,' Holmes said. 'It was apparent from my observations of you and Crowhurst, when we were all sat talking, that there was a clear and present danger towards you. That is why I outed you when I did. I did not know it then, but I suspect Crowhurst had discovered you'd received those missing papers, since this group must have realised that Green had passed them on.'

'That makes sense,' Finch said. 'His attitude changed towards me soon after. When I could no longer hide my fears from Her Majesty, she commanded I tell her what was wrong. So I did. Everything. She wasn't convinced she could help, and truthfully I suspect she might have thought me a little hysterical. Once I showed her the papers that revealed there was a plan to replace her with the Prince of Wales, Her Majesty soon came around.'

'The Prince is away to Germany isn't he?' Holmes asked.

'Yes, and I have nothing linking any of this to him,' Finch pointed out.

'That is *some* good news,' I said.

Finch appeared to agree with me. 'Once Her Majesty saw those documents, we both recognised neither of us could take it to the government. I didn't know who to trust – but the Queen, it seems, trusted you. It was Her Majesty who decided on the plan to entice you.'

Holmes nodded. 'Her strategy was a wise one.'

'I played my part. And I made it obvious it could only have been *me* who'd taken the stone. But no one could accuse me without proof. When Inspector Gregson arrived and initially interviewed me, I saw he was suspicious. I thought to confide in him, but then the Home Secretary arrived here and that ended that. That night when I arrived home, I noticed Gregson had put men to watching my house – policemen are easy to spot. It caused those other fellows to disappear. Those policemen actually made me safer.'

'And once Crowhurst was dispatched to collect me,' Holmes said, 'you handed the Queen the stone and then went to your office to wait to discover what I would do next?'

'Exactly. I knew she intended to give it to you. When you immediately outed me, I assumed it came with a plan. I saw how you'd worked those police and military men. I watched as you had them running around, but they were doing nothing to find me. As time went on, I felt more and more you were on my side, but then you let Crowhurst go. And now, I hardly know *what* to think.'

'It is not a betrayal,' Holmes assured him. 'Your strategy might have seemed solid, but it wasn't. Crowhurst is one of the miscreants, and I need them *all* if I am to bring this affair to a close. Do you understand?'

'I do now,' Finch nodded. 'I think now that you're involved, these fellows might look to change their plans?'

Holmes appeared to agree. 'Yes. But I suspect whatever the plan is, it can't be easily modified. If the intention is to abduct the Queen, that is no easy task to arrange. The method by which such a thing...' Holmes growled. 'I'm a fool. Crowhurst told me. You told me also, and I missed it.'

'Missed what?' I asked.

'Her Majesty is going to Osborne House.'

'As she always does this time of year,' Finch said, frowning.

'It will happen tonight,' Holmes stated.

'No, she should already be there,' Finch declared.

Holmes shook his head. 'Crowhurst told us Her Majesty will leave from Portsmouth *tonight*,' he said. 'There was a delay because her boat had some maintenance issues. Her Majesty will be travelling to Portsmouth later this evening.'

The major's face whitened. 'Meaning they've possibly done something to her boat?'

'I cannot say for certain.' Holmes gave me a grim look. 'But since Sir Henry's accident appears related to a boat...'

'Good lord!'

'If we leave now, we'll have a little under four hours before she sails,' I said, checking my watch.

'We might make it to Portsmouth in that time, but we'll need Scotland Yard to commission a special train for us.'

'My man should be back soon,' Finch offered. 'He'll have word on Crowhurst at least.'

Holmes seemed pleased. 'Thank you, Major. You have assisted me greatly. Now,' he said, standing, 'we have little time, so—'

Whatever Holmes was about to say was suddenly lost in the sound of a gunshot reverberating through the enclosed space between us. I could only stare in shock as Major Finch crumpled to the ground. Although my instinct was to assist him, Holmes had other plans. After he'd kicked the table over between us, he pulled me down behind it – just as a second shot rang out. To my horror, I watched it hit the table and breathed a sigh as a metal layer between the wood stopped it from coming through and hitting me in the head.

Holmes let out a blast on a whistle just as a third shot thudded into the table.

Chapter Ten

'There's no way anyone could break in without our knowing it.'

Sherlock Holmes and I could do little else but crouch behind that heavy table as the shots continued to hit it. My friend had blown another sharp blast on his whistle, just as a fourth, fifth and sixth round hit. When the seventh thudded into the grouping, Holmes tapped my shoulder.

'That's it,' Holmes said, pointing to the door. 'Eight rounds. Depending on how quickly he can change a magazine, we'll have time to get behind that wall.'

I nodded, and we both scooted as fast as we could in a crouch to the stone wall at the back of the room, and fell down behind it.

'Fortunately for us,' Holmes said, 'this part of the complex is as old as the White Tower. Those rounds won't penetrate here.'

'We're lucky that old table could withstand them,' I said. 'I thought for sure we were done for.'

Holmes nodded. 'It's a semi-modern heavy oak with draw leaves,' he said. 'There's a thick iron lining between the base and bottom leave. It not only gives the table its weight and sturdiness, but along with the top, makes for an excellent barrier against black-powder rifle ammunition.'

'It's fortunate they're still using those older Lee-Metford rifles.'

Holmes nodded. 'With their poor sighting-in, it renders those rifles woefully inaccurate at range. Add in those black-powder cartridges and the hard angle our shooter had to reach, along with poor light – the science was on our side.'

'Although not for poor Major Finch,' I said. It was apparent now he'd been killed.

'Sadly no. I calculate from their angle and the depth of penetration into the wood, our shooter is above us somewhere southeast. One tower along that corner. Possibly Wakefield.'

We sat for a moment longer and waited, and as no more rounds fired, I began to relax. Holmes peered around the wall and I momentarily expected to hear a shot and to see my friend crumple as Finch had done, but of course Holmes had calculated the odds and already decided the risk was marginal. I heard heavy boots and yelling, followed by a general hum of activity that accompanies a group of military and policemen when they suddenly find themselves able to spend their pent-up energies. Holmes blew his whistle again and those voices and boots grew louder, as a few men came to investigate. Holmes and I quickly cleared away the barricade of furniture that Finch had used to block off the door, which we pulled open before shouting to attract attention. Soon, two guardsmen appeared in the doorway, followed by a pair of constables. The guard aimed his rifle at us, whilst a constable came forwards with up a lamp.

'Stand and be recognised,' I heard the guardsman yell.

'It's Mr Holmes and Dr Watson,' Gregson said, pushing his way through. 'Are either of you injured?'

'No,' Holmes said. 'But Finch took a shot to the head. He's dead.'

The inspector paused at the doorway. 'Those shots were aimed at this room?'

'At *us*,' I said.

'Where do you imagine—?'

'A tower on the southeast corner,' Holmes said. 'I suspect either the Bloody Tower or Wakefield – but better to have the guardsmen search. I believe it's the Guard Captain, so send the sergeant here.'

Gregson pointed to him, and the sergeant made to leave, but Holmes stopped him. 'Alive, if at all possible. We need answers.' The sergeant nodded, pointed to two others, and they bolted away.

'So, you'd found him then?' Gregson asked, peering into the room.

'We'd just heard his story,' I said.

'Which was interrupted,' Holmes added, turning to the policeman. 'Brighten that lamp and bring it in here, will you?'

The constable stepped forwards, but I stopped him and Holmes from entering.

'There's a man with a rifle still out there,' I cautioned. 'You're not seriously going back in?'

Holmes nodded. 'He hasn't fired a single shot since he emptied his magazine.'

'That doesn't mean he isn't—'

'The fellow was *only* interested in Finch,' Holmes pointed out. 'Since he is dead, it seems clear he considers his job done.'

'You can't know that for certain,' I growled. 'Why did he continue to empty his magazine if one shot was all he needed to make?'

'There is a logical answer for it. Time. Our sniper may not have been confident that his first shot instantly killed Finch, and therefore kept us too concerned with our own safety to assist him.'

'Where he quickly bled to death,' I said, shaking my head.

'Exactly. Now, step aside, please, Watson. Constable, stand behind me as I enter, and remain that way as I go through the room.'

I held up my hands and obeyed, stepping aside, and Holmes, with the constable in tow, began examining every part of the room.

'What is he looking for?' Gregson asked as we slipped in behind them, careful to keep as much wall between us, and the window on the far side.

'The paperwork Finch said he had to prove his story was true, I expect.'

'And what story is that?' Gregson asked. It was obvious he didn't enjoy being the last to know – a feeling I understood well. I recounted it, which helped to reinforce it for when I made my notes. Gregson listened intently. When I arrived at Major Finch's conclusions regarding the Queen, and the revelations Crowhurst was working for the Home Secretary, who appeared to be the chief architect behind the affair, Inspector Gregson stared at me in stunned silence.

'That is… a remarkable story,' Gregson said carefully. His expression suggested he was struggling to find the entire story credible. 'And Mr Holmes had this missing stone on him all along, eh?'

I nodded. 'The Queen gave it to him when we arrived.'

'And it was a fake, you say?'

'Apparently so. A lump of ordinary rose quartz, so he said.'

Gregson sighed. 'And now you say Crowhurst, who I admit I didn't much care for, was playing us?'

'That's what Finch says.'

Gregson frowned. 'And he's an agent of some group of villains led by the Home Secretary?'

'Indeed.'

'Well, that doesn't sound at all wild,' Gregson murmured. 'Let's hope Mr Holmes finds this evidence because without it, I doubt we'll get far with my superintendent. He'll want something pretty big to even contemplate making a move against the Home Secretary.'

I understood what he meant, and was about to comment, when a snarl from Holmes caused me to look away. When he approached us, I could tell he had been unsuccessful.

'Nothing?' Gregson asked.

Holmes shook his head. 'Not a thing.'

'He didn't leave it elsewhere?' I asked. 'At his house,

maybe?'

'Unlikely. I don't believe Finch would leave anything of value there, since someone might break in and take it. No, he would have kept those papers close.'

Gregson frowned. 'My best men watch that house,' he said. 'There's no way anyone could break in without our knowing it.'

'Inspector, I could be in and out and your men would never know,' Holmes growled.

Gregson raised an eyebrow. 'Perhaps he left them in his office?'

Holmes sighed. 'Do you honestly think I haven't thought of that, Inspector?' my friend snapped. He swallowed his growing irritation. 'Forgive me. Finch would have put them somewhere close. Somewhere he knew no one would think to look.'

'That's fair,' I said. 'He was seeing conspiracies in every shadow.'

'Exactly. Those papers were the *only* thing that proved his story. There were at least two people here who wanted them – possibly a third in his accomplice.'

'You think his accomplice was part of this gang?' I asked.

'No, but the more I ponder on this strange affair, the more I think there's another agency involved – and this agency's agenda appears aligned with ours.'

Gregson sighed. 'This is all becoming difficult to keep track of.'

'It's perfectly simple, Inspector. One group of people is attempting to subvert justice and potentially disrupt the affairs of the Crown, a second group is attempting to thwart them – and in the middle was Major Finch.'

'That makes a little more sense. How'd he get himself involved?'

Holmes smiled. 'Rather foolishly,' he said.

'So, we have to search the Tower for these missing papers when the Queen could be in danger,' I growled.

'One problem at a time, Watson,' Holmes snapped. 'Now

please, will you both cease your conversations? I must think.' He then sat himself on the floor and closed his eyes.

I knew to remain silent, but Gregson – who did not know how difficult Holmes could get if interrupted from deep concentration – whispered something to me.

'Finch's accomplice is due back soon?'

'Yes,' I breathed.

'Maybe he can shed light on things?'

'Possibly,' I hissed, gesturing that we really should be quiet.

'At the very least, he might explain what he wanted in the guard room?'

'Inspector!' Holmes snarled. I winced at the rebuke that was sure to follow, but Holmes surprised me by jumping to his feet and grabbing and shaking the inspector's hand. 'The guard room!'

'What of it?' Gregson asked, startled.

'I know where Finch hid those papers,' Holmes said. 'Quickly, both of you, we have little time.'

We followed Sherlock Holmes outside, he holding the constable's lantern. He led us to King's House, to a small tearoom and a gift stall. Holmes handed the lantern to me and made his way to the stall. I observed various books, maps, and children's wooden toys, but Holmes ignored all that memorabilia in favour of a display full of stuffed bears in uniform. The inspector and I joined stood to one side as he began a thorough examining of each bear, carefully placing them aside until he picked up one which caused him to give a triumphant shout.

Holmes turned it to us. 'Here is it!'

'What do you want a child's bear for?' Gregson asked.

'I have no interest in the bear,' Holmes replied, taking a small knife from his pocket and plunging it into the soft toy's belly. 'It's what's inside.' He cut it open and pulled it apart to reveal a roll of papers. 'Voila!'

Holmes quickly verified their contents and whistled. 'No wonder Crowhurst was prepared to kill to find these.'

'How did you know to look here, of all places?' Gregson asked, frowning.

'It was *you* who gave me the hint, Inspector,' Holmes said, smiling. 'You mentioned the guard house. Finch's confederate took several things from it. Including a sewing kit and cotton wadding.'

'And from that you reasoned he used those items to hide his papers in a child's toy bear?' Gregson chuckled. 'I wouldn't have considered that.'

'Well,' Holmes said, seemingly satisfied. 'Now that we have them, I see why Finch was as terrified as he was.'

A shout of challenge happened nearby, followed by the pounding of boots on stone. We exited to find a guardsman coming our way.

'What is it?' Gregson asked.

'The captain's been spotted,' the young military man said. 'He's gone into Wakefield Tower.'

'Well, after him, man,' Gregson said, and we followed him as he ran off.

We were standing on the lower level of Wakefield Tower, and about to ascend, when we heard several voices issuing orders, followed by a cry of alarm – and finally a shot. We all bounded up the stairs where we found the Guard Captain had taken his own life.

Evidently, after being confronted by his men, he refused to let them take him into custody, and I suspect he couldn't bear the thought of taking any of their lives. So he took his own life to end the problem.

'I'm sure he thought it was the honourable way out,' I mused.

'He murdered a man in cold blood,' Holmes retorted. 'He doesn't get to be a hero.'

'We don't know what he was told by Crowhurst,' I pointed out. 'He could have thought he was following a lawful order.'

'Then he would have no reason to kill himself,' Holmes growled.

I stuttered because Holmes was correct.

'I suspect he killed himself to save his master any embarrassment. He *was* one of the named members of this gang. There's nothing more we can do here.'

A whistle blew, and Gregson turned. 'What now?'

'I suspect Finch's companion has returned,' Holmes offered.

When we made it outside, we discovered two constables escorting the fellow to us.

'This man says he needs to speak with Mr Holmes,' one said.

My friend stepped forwards. 'I am Sherlock Holmes.'

'I know,' the fellow said. 'Call me Smith, if you like. Where is Major Finch?'

'Finch is dead,' Gregson said.

'I'm very sorry to hear that,' Smith said, and appeared to mean it. 'Did you speak with him?'

Holmes nodded. 'Briefly. It appears your master had some particular concerns.'

Smith smiled. 'Valid ones, Mr Holmes. But to be clear, I didn't work for Finch.'

'And just who do you work for, *Smith*?'

Smith inclined his head. 'Shall we say… an interested party?'

'Interested in what?' Gregson asked.

'Many things,' Smith offered with a smile. 'At this moment, in safeguarding our Queen. Did Major Finch pass anything on to you, Mr Holmes? Items for safe keeping? Papers perhaps?'

The inspector coughed, but Holmes quickly answered. 'Major Finch died before he could do that,' he replied.

'By the Guard Captain?' Smith asked.

Holmes nodded. 'You seem very well informed.'

"I knew something like this might happen if I left him. It's a blow. I've been working with Finch for a week attempting to recover those papers. It is hard for him to trust anyone. I thought he might come to trust me. I really need to find them.'

'Never mind those papers,' Holmes said. 'They aren't going anywhere. When the time comes, they will surface. Now, tell me what happened to the colonel?'

'He caught a cab to Nine Elms. I think it's clear he's heading to Portsmouth.'

Holmes was thoughtful. 'As I suspected. Do we know if Her Majesty has left Buckingham Palace yet?'

'She has,' Smith acknowledged. 'A little over hour ago.'

'Then we *must* hire a special,' Holmes said. 'I assume you or your benefactor *can* arrange that?'

Smith nodded. 'There's one waiting for us now. My benefactor, as you call him, is eager that you should come.'

'Then we should not keep him waiting,' Holmes mused.

Smith chuckled. 'If we hurry, we should make it to Gosport in a little over two hours.'

My friend checked his pocket watch. 'That'll put us around an hour *behind* Crowhurst.'

Smith shook his head. 'Crowhurst caught the Southampton train. It was waiting at the station when he arrived. Our special should actually close that gap by thirty minutes.'

Holmes seemed satisfied by that.

'Shall we go?' Smith asked.

'Yes,' Holmes said. 'Come, Watson, Inspector.'

'Now wait a moment,' Gregson said. 'I can't go bounding off to wherever it is you're going. There are two dead men here. I have to take care of that.'

Holmes frowned. 'I really don't like the idea of leaving without you, Inspector. You *should* be there at the end. I insist upon it. Can one of your men not fetch another inspector to take charge here?'

Gregson seemed moved by Holmes's request. I admit I thought it very uncharacteristic. Gregson gave him an appreciative nod, then turned to the nearest constable and issued the orders. While Smith collected one of the police carriages, I turned to Holmes.

'That was a very personal plea you just made.'

'He knows how to do as he's told,' Holmes replied, 'and having a policeman helps ground the military types.'

When Smith arrived with the carriage, we were all on our way to Nine Elms Station.

* * *

As Smith had explained, there was a special train with one carriage waiting for us as we entered the station. As soon as we boarded, the train immediately powered away. The carriage looked more like a buffet car than those used for passengers. Smith left us to congregate with several men gathered around a table. My observation suggested these men might be ex-military, as they were plain clothed. Holmes smiled at me and pointed to the end of the carriage.

'Something calamitous must have happened,' Holmes said as he moved forwards, 'to force *you* onto a train.'

Gregson and I moved up behind Holmes as he spoke. A familiar face poked out from around a seat, and smiled at us.

'Sherlock!' the rather bulky Mycroft Holmes said. 'I gather you're *not* surprised to see me?'

Holmes shook his head. 'Once I understood who Smith was, I suspected you were behind things. This government special rather clinched it.'

Mycroft Holmes grinned. 'This train will take us to Royal Clarence Yard in Gosport. That is where Her Majesty will board her boat for her journey across the Solent to her house at Osborne on the Isle of Wight.'

'Have we sent a message to ensure she doesn't board the boat?' Holmes asked.

Mycroft Holmes nodded. 'But it may not reach her in time. It is therefore imperative that *we* do.'

'How long have you been involved in this case?' I asked. Holmes had said Mycroft's role in the government was unique. He practically had his own mandate – so I understood.

'Involved, Doctor?' Mycroft frowned. 'I'm forever *involved*, but not always by choice. These things come across my desk from time to time. I suppose you could say I've been active for a week now.' Mycroft Holmes grunted. 'And I shall be perfectly content to revert to torpid as soon as this case is concluded.'

Holmes chuckled as he took out his pipe, then stuffed and lit it.

'What put you onto Crowhurst?' my friend asked.

'That poor fellow Green,' Mycroft said, sipping a glass of whiskey he'd collected from his table. 'When Scotland Yard found him dead, I was asked to look into things. His death and the circumstances that led to it caused me to suspect something deeper. I had these fellows,' he said, pointing to the men on the train, 'do a little reconnaissance for me.'

'They're government men?' I asked.

'You could say they're part of an organisation of law enforcement experts, and just leave it at that.'

'They don't *look* like policemen,' Gregson said.

'I'm thrilled to hear you say so, Inspector,' Mycroft replied. 'Because they aren't.'

Holmes let out a cloud of smoke. 'You're aware of all Finch's concerns, of course?'

'Of course,' Mycroft said, nodding 'We've been aware of the Home Secretary's traitorous behaviour for some time. It wasn't until this fellow Green poked a stick into a rather active nest of wasps that the extent of those activities emerged. Now, one cannot simply remove a minster from Parliament, but a Prime Minister *can* shuffle them into another job. We suggested it, but the Home Secretary has powerful influential men behind him. The Prime Minister, therefore, will not act without proof. My friends here went looking and discovered Green had beaten us to it. What's more, this gang got to him before we could, and they killed him for his trouble. We lost track of the papers, but Smith is a cunning devil. He went through the records and discovered a link to Green that others had failed to find.'

Holmes nodded. 'Major Finch. They served together in Afghanistan.'

'Right. And once we knew that, I selected Smith to work on helping Finch.'

'But the major was reluctant?'

Mycroft sighed. 'Crowhurst and his men caused Finch significant psychological difficulties, Sherlock. The death of his friend, Green, caused an even greater strain on his mind. Those emotional concerns kept him in a heightened state of agitation.'

'We saw,' Holmes stated. 'Finch could no longer distinguish friend from foe.'

'Exactly. I wanted Smith to work on him, to help him re-adjust. And he befriended him enough to gain the knowledge we'd all be hoping for. That what evidence Green had discovered did not die with him. It was out there, somewhere. We need those papers, and that's when I thought about you.'

Sherlock Holmes nodded. 'And after Crowhurst arranged Sir Henry's accident, *you* suggested the means by which Her Majesty might pique my interest?'

Mycroft smiled. 'I knew it would have to be something extraordinary, or you'd probably not take her seriously. Sir Henry survived, but we had to keep him apart from the Queen, since time was running out to discover the fullness of their plan, and to stop it. *I* knew it would be impossible for me to influence you, as I felt sure you'd not have been so convinced by Crowhurst's pleas had I done so. He isn't as idiotic as he makes himself out to be, Sherlock.' Mycroft winked at me. 'So, I persuaded the Queen to. She involved Finch, and the rest you know. But I suspect you saw through it all quickly enough?'

I admit it pleased me to learn that Mycroft had used my friend in a similar way to how he'd earlier used me.

Holmes chuckled. 'I recognised the purpose behind it, yes.'

'And you suspected my involvement from the beginning?'

'Not from the beginning,' Holmes replied. 'But, we aren't brothers for nothing,' Holmes pointed out. 'I saw the truth after I contemplated on my conversation with Her Majesty.'

This apparently pleased the older Holmes. 'Splendid, and it appears, despite what you told Smith earlier, you've found what we need.' Mycroft held out his hand. 'I'll take those papers that are upsetting the lining of your nice jacket now, Sherlock, if you don't mind.'

My friend smiled as he pulled the papers out and handed them over to his brother.

'Thank you.' Mycroft scanned them and beamed. 'Most gratifying. We have *everything* we need.'

My friend then checked his watch. 'We'll arrive in—'

'Approximately one hour and fifteen minutes,' finished Mycroft Holmes.

It was amusing for them both to finish each other's sentences – not so much for anyone attempting to follow their conversations.

'Why don't you pour yourself a drink and relax whilst I read through these papers?'

* * *

The train made it to Royal Clarence Yard a little earlier than either Holmes expected, because of the hard work of the train coalman and driver. The group disembarked behind the Holmes brothers, where Mycroft took the lead. An officer and guard detail met him on approach.

'Mr Mycroft,' the officer said. 'Her Majesty arrived thirty minutes ago, and they'll be settling her onboard as we speak.'

Mycroft Holmes turned to us. 'Sherlock, secure Her Majesty first,' he said. 'Anything else is secondary.'

Holmes nodded.

'I will speak with the Navel Chief,' Mycroft said. 'All this activity is souring my stomach.' He then turned away from us.

Holmes chuckled as he led us to the dock.

'Right. Let's get aboard that ship and find Her Majesty,' Inspector Gregson said, pointing to a group of sailors. 'You men, come with us.'

The inspector was about to lead those naval recruits onto the boat when Holmes stopped him.

'One moment, please. I need to make a quick examination of the ground before you all destroy it.' Holmes dropped to his hands and knees and scrutinised the path all the way along to the gangplank. He then made a survey of the visible sections of Her Majesty's boat, and when he was finished, he stood and nodded. 'Thank you, Inspector, you may continue now,' he said.

Inspector Gregson led those naval men onto the path, and they soon barrelled along the gangplank and disappeared into the boat.

'Aren't we going to follow?' I asked.

Holmes shook his head. 'We shall wait and see what Gregson discovers first.'

I frowned. It was a little unusual for Holmes not to be in the lead, but if I knew anything at all, I knew he had a plan. So I waited beside him in silence. His eyes, I noticed, continually scanned the upper deck of the boat. Something caught his attention, and he gave a sharp blast from his whistle, attracting the attention of the naval men on a tug with a searchlight.

'You there,' Holmes called out. 'Shine your beacon on the upper deck aft. Quickly.'

The light appeared to single out what Holmes had seen. It was a man, and he immediately covered his eyes, and seemed to drop something as the light blinded him.

'Who is it?' I asked.

Holmes ignored me and cupped his mouth. 'Gregson,' he yelled, gaining the inspector's attentions. 'It's Crowhurst!'

I watched as a group of men ran towards the man Holmes identified as Crowhurst, but before they reached him, something caused them all to stop. I grabbed a pair of binoculars from a midshipman and saw Crowhurst yelling at Gregson and the others. All the time Crowhurst held a revolver – *my* revolver – to his head. There was a lot of confused yelling, and I could not easily tell who was saying what. I then observed two men rush the colonel from the side, and that was when I heard a shot and watched as Crowhurst dropped. From this distance I couldn't tell if one of the naval men had shot him, or if he'd taken his own life. I looked to Holmes expecting him to be startled, but his expression actually surprised me. Before I could say a word, he gave a bellowed warning, which was echoed onboard by several cries of alarm on the deck. I watched as Gregson frantically waved at the men who started running towards him at speed. I wondered what had caused such agitation, and was about to ask Holmes, when a rumble and flash lit the boat up, shortly followed by an enormous explosion that came from the ship's port side, upper deck aft, the force of which rained debris onto the dock, the gangplanks, and the small tug boat that was pulling away beside. Those of us ashore instantly retreated to a safer distance, just as a second explosion occurred.

'Her Majesty!' I exclaimed, leaping forwards.

'She's not onboard,' Holmes said, firmly taking my arm.

'But where *is* she, then?'

Sherlock Holmes let go of my arm. His eyes sparkled. 'We shall find her.' I turned to see a large section of the ship engulfed in fire. The cracking sounds increased until a small section collapsed.

'She's done for,' I remarked.

'Let's hope this boat is the only significant casualty,' Holmes said. 'Come, Watson. We don't have a moment to lose.'

* * *

Sherlock Holmes led us away from the quayside towards a wharf where other boats were moored. He turned us toward an assortment of outbuildings, all the time keeping us in the shadows. Eventually, we came to an open concourse that contained several boathouses. My friend then pointed to a wall, which we quickly crouch-ran to. We paused there, kneeling in the long grass, while Holmes peered around one end. He looked back and made a clear gesture towards one building. When he seemed satisfied I'd understood his meaning, he dashed away, heading straight for it, and I followed – veering off to one side and hugging the shadows – as Holmes led us deeper into the dark twisted pathways beyond.

Holmes stopped for a moment, and dropped to a knee to

examine the ground. He then stood, and pointed towards a path between two buildings, which we swiftly made it to – ducking underneath a large window – and hiding ourselves in the inset dark entrance of the tall building.

'Take this,' Holmes whispered, pressing a revolver into my hand.

'Where—'

'From Smith on the train,' Holmes said. 'I think your revolver is sadly lost. Hopefully this will make for a suitable replacement.'

I tested the weight and turned it over. It was newer and had seen less action, and the sentimental part of it would always be missing, but despite all of that, I was grateful to have it in my hand.

The calamity at the boat had drawn everyone to it. The horrible ordeal those people faced, along with the challenges a burning and exploding boat brings when moored near other boats, with flames carried upon the wind, was not lost on me. Holmes, I knew, would only attune himself to what mattered to his case. I shook off the distractions and followed as he led us to a similar-looking building, where he repeated the same set of actions I'd observed earlier. At the third building, he hissed and had us hug the wall tighter. I observed the moonlight as it danced across the expanse of his widening eyes. He held that expression of suppressed excitement, which often came when he'd accomplished a goal.

Sherlock Holmes then removed his own revolver from his pocket and cocked it. He gestured towards the door and gave me a three count. I waited until my friend opened the door far enough for us to sneak through, and he took point. We traversed the dirt floor as noiselessly as we could, and came to another doorway, where the door was opened a crack, and from behind we heard muffled voices.

Holmes pointed, and I could see a carriage sitting in the centre of the room with two beautiful black stallions at its head. It was obvious by the light filtering through the shuttered windows that someone occupied the carriage. Again, we sneaked through the doorway, and this time Holmes and I crouch-ran to either side of the rear of that carriage. We each came quietly along one side – the soft dirt dampening our footfalls as we went – meeting at the harness at the front where a man stood smoking a fat cigar.

'That'll do,' Holmes said to the startled fellow who found the steel of my friend's revolver pressed deep into his neck. 'Watson, disarm him.'

I ducked under the harness behind the horses and did as he instructed, keeping my eyes on the fellow at all times, whilst Holmes took a step back from him.

'The game's up, *Mr* Home Secretary,' my friend said.

'Who the devil are you?'

'This is Mr Sherlock Holmes,' I said, keeping him covered with my revolver as I manoeuvred around the horses. 'Perhaps you've heard of him?'

'Oh, lord,' the Home Secretary moaned, then he threw himself at Holmes, knocking him to the dirt, his revolver lost under the carriage. They wrestled together as I approached and attempted to pull the fellow off, but he was as strong as an ox. His elbow soon had me spinning away and I fell backwards into the dirt. I watched with growing alarm, as I scrambled up, to see the Home Secretary apparently get the better of my friend. He'd manoeuvred Holmes onto his back and used those large hands of his to grab him by the throat. I saw the fellow's face turned almost purple as he yelled terrible oaths, his spittle flying as he put all his effort into strangling the life out of my friend. I quicky put an end to it by pistol-whipping the back of his head. Holmes gave an audible intake of breath as I rolled the fellow off and laid him unconscious in the dirt.

'Thank you,' the hoarse voice of my friend said as I assisted him to his feet. 'Help me secure this villain, will you?' Holmes stood, wheezing, and handed me the coil of rope I'd observed him collect at the dock.

'Tie his hands behind him tightly.'

Holmes settled his breathing as he turned his attention to the carriage, bending over to collect his revolver. He then went to the door. 'You may come out now, Your Majesty,' Holmes said. 'We have the fellow under arrest.'

The door of the Royal Carriage opened and Sherlock Holmes assisted Queen Victoria down the steps, her three ladies-in-waiting following her out.

The Queen briefly eyed her abductor, then turned to us. 'We should like to leave this hideous place now, Mr Holmes,' she said.

Epilogue

I should like to start this epilogue by paying tribute to the late Major John Finch, who was posthumously awarded the Victoria Cross by Her Majesty for his service and defence of the Crown. We hardly had a moment to reflect on his loss during the case, but many months have since gone by and both Holmes and I were thrilled to see his name added to the honours list.

Shortly after we'd rescued the Queen, Mycroft Holmes, along with Naval Command, took control of the situation – and the Home Secretary. Someone had rigged Her Majesty's boat with explosives, and the plan was to set them off during the crossing and give the impression the Queen had gone down with the ship. The intention was never to kill Her Majesty, but abduct her and take her abroad somewhere, where she would live out her days in isolation. Holmes recognised that in order to accomplish such a feat, others of this conspiracy must have been on the boat – which meant they must also have been a part of the senior naval crew. It did not take the Holmes brothers long to discover those traitors and add them to an already growing bag.

The entire affair came undone when Sherlock Holmes

recognised the Queen was not onboard, explaining, amongst other things, that her standard hadn't been raised – something always done when the monarch comes aboard. My friend also said he saw no shoe impressions at the dock to correspond with Her Majesty coming from any one of the carriages that had pulled up beside the private gangplank. The Queen had entered her carriage with her ladies-in-waiting after she'd disembarked the train, but had then been taken directly to the boat-shed where Holmes and I rescued her.

Colonel Crowhurst, upon seeing Holmes and Gregson, knew his game was up and opted to kill himself, rather than be taken for questioning – as the Guard Captain at the Tower had also done. Crowhurst had accidentally dropped an unstable block of explosives when the searchlight hit him, which he fell against after killing himself, and that caused a chain reaction ending with the ship exploding and burning at the dock. Those that could calmly evacuated, including Inspector Gregson, who'd stayed the longest to ensure everyone got out. Aside from three ship hands that were caught in the initial explosions, almost the entire sixty-strong crew made it safely to shore.

Once the evidence was placed before the Home Secretary whom Mycroft considered the kingpin, he agreed to give up other members of the conspiracy. These included several key members of government, and a senior courtier at Buckingham Palace. The thing was so wide ranging, a special trial under blackout was arranged. There were legal conditions placed upon those records with stiff penalties advised for anyone who breached them.

In order to publish the story, I had to change the record to ensure I complied with my legal duties. Almost all the names within are changed to some degree. I have not disclosed the year, nor have the names of any government officials – save for Mycroft Holmes and Sir Henry Ponsonby – found their way into the narrative, leaving those individuals, such as the Home Secretary, only identified by their titles.

Sherlock and Mycroft Holmes discovered another arm of this group of anarchists, and with their help – along with the records Major Finch had gathered, and the detailed information the Home Secretary had supplied to save his neck from the hangman – the police were able to successfully round them all up.

'It is strange,' I mused as I paused my writing.

'Hmm?' Holmes said, removing his pipe from his mouth. 'What is?'

'Well, how we started believing we'd be investigating a jewel theft, only to discover it was really all to do with a plot against the Queen.'

Holmes nodded. 'One can only hope every case will turn so delightfully unconventional.'

'Yes,' I said, as I opened the box and reviewed the beautiful British Empire Medal Her Majesty had awarded me. 'Have you decided if you'll accept the knighthood?' I asked him.

'I have declined it twice before. I would think they'd eventually stop asking,' Holmes said, dropping his pipe on the side-table. 'These things mean little to me, as you know. The work is my only reward.' He reminded me often that he had never needed trinkets, but I inwardly chuckled this time, as I watched him stare into the fire and unconsciously adjust the pink-diamond cufflink Her Majesty had made for him from a stone in her collection.

'I know *that* look,' my friend said.

'I don't know what you mean.'

'I'm not sure that's entirely true,' Holmes remarked with a chuckle. 'You have the look you *always* have when you've completed a new tale of our exploits together. You know that you'll be unable to publish it?'

'Maybe not now, but at some point in the future.'

'It'll have to be a number of decades into the future, possibly after we're all dust.'

I nodded.

'So, what do you intend to call this one, then?'

'In honour of Her Majesty and Major Finch,' I said, 'I intend to call it *The King's Diamond*.'

Holmes nodded and, with a twinkle in his eye, he said, 'An apt title, since as with most of your work of late, this too is *mostly* fiction.'

THE END

* * * *

Coming March 2023

The Watson Chronicles

When Miss Violet Montgomery, daughter of late Hatton Garden Jeweller Harry Montgomery, writes to Sherlock Holmes asking for his help in solving a theft from her family home, the famous detective takes little persuading to agree to the case. Unbeknownst to Miss Violet, six months previously – and a month before her father's death – Harry Montgomery had written a similar letter to Holmes, who was abroad at the time and unable to assist. Harry and Violet's pleas share a common thread, as each refer to the loss of a curious red pin...

Available for pre-order on Amazon

Coming 2023

The Watson Chronicles

Christopher D. Abbott, Keith R.A. DeCandido, Michael Jan Friedman and Aaron Rosenberg team up to bring you another stunning collection of Sherlock Holmes adventures.

A pea-souper descending over London brings with it many villainous activities hidden deep within those thickly yellow-hazed streets, and for Sherlock Holmes and his faithful friend Dr. John Watson, it often provides cases to test the detective's intellectual prowess and his affinity for the unusual and bizarre.

Pull up a chair by the fire and prepare yourself as Abbott, DeCandido, Friedman, and Rosenberg present you with *more* cases…by candlelight.

Available for pre-order on Amazon

Soulcat
A Feline Memoir

Amy wrote a love letter... a note to the love of her life.

Only, Molly never read it. Even if she'd been alive when it was written, failing eyesight would have prevented her from making out the words.

Besides which, she was a cat. And cats can't read.

No ordinary Feline, Molly lived a life full of challenge and adventure, determined not to let gradual blindness hold her back.

This is that letter and - against all the odds - Molly's long lost memoirs...

Available on Kindle, Kindle Unlimited and at Soulcat.co.uk

"Rosenberg's tongue-in-cheek approach charms, creating an endearing, hirsute hero. Readers are sure to be entertained."
— Publishers Weekly

YETI LEFT HOME

Aaron Rosenberg

Small-Town Yeti, Big-City Problems

Peaceful, unassuming Wylie Kang—a Yeti with an appreciation for more *human* creature comforts—lives a quiet life in his self-built sanctuary on the outskirts of Embarrass, Minnesota. But when violent dreams disturb his peace, and a series of strange murders plague the area, a Hunter comes to town, nosing after Wylie's trail.

Fleeing pursuit, Wylie packs up his truck and heads for the Twin Cities, hoping to lose himself in the urban jungle, only to find a thriving supernatural community.

Just as he begins to settle in—with the help of some new-found friends—he discovers the bloodshed has followed... as has the Hunter.

Can Wylie catch the killer, before the Hunter catches him?

Available through all commercial booksellers

NeoParadoxa
https://especbooks.square.site

About the Author

Christopher is a Reader's Favorite award-winning author of crime, fantasy, science-fiction, and horror.

Described by New York Times Bestseller Michael Jan Friedman as "an up-and-coming fantasy voice", and compared to Roger Zelazny's best work, Abbott's Songs of the Osirian series of works brings a bold re-telling of Ancient Egyptian mythology. Abbott presents a fresh view of deities we know, such as Horus, Osiris, and Anubis. He weaves the godlike magic through musical poetry, giving these wonderfully tragic and deeply flawed "gods" different perspective, all the while increasing their mysteriousness.

His Sherlock Holmes stories, published in the Watson Chronicles Series, have been recognised by readers and peers alike as faithfully authentic to the original Conan Doyle. In 2022, after publishing seven individual Watson Chronicle stories, Christopher teamed up with prolific authors Michael Jan Friedman and Aaron Rosenberg to add a collection of Holmes short stories to the series.

Christopher has published with Crazy8Press and written for major media outlets, including ScreenRant.

Info@cdanabbott.com
cdanabbott@gmail.com

and find him online at:

www.facebook.com/cdanabbott
www.twitter.com/cdanabbott
www.instagram.com/cdanabbott

and at his website:

cdanabbott.com

Original Mystery & Suspense

Join Dr. Straay as he investigates the mysterious murders of Sir Laurence Gregson, and Dr. Simon Chandrix, in these classic Agatha Christie-styled murder mystery stories

Available on Amazon

Sci-Fi - Horror

PROGENITOR
CHRISTOPHER D ABBOTT

More To Fear Than Fear Itself

When a horde of towering creatures wreaks havoc on FDR's Washington D.C., no one–including the president–knows where they came from. A desperate group of survivors makes it to Fort Detrick, where they seek refuge from the devastation. They think they're safe there. After all, It's FDR's state-of-the-art maximum-security facility. But relief turns to horror, as they find they've locked themselves in with a more hideous threat than the one they left behind.

CRAZY 8 PRESS

crazy8press.com

The Watson Chronicles

At the end of his own birthday celebration, Major Peterson shocks his seven guests by leaving the party, going into his study, and apparently shooting himself.

Inspector Delaware discovers conflicting evidence, however, and calls for help from Sherlock Holmes. Upon their arrival, Holmes tells Watson he believes there's more to Peterson's death than the evidence might suggest. Still, the facts continue to show that Peterson committed suicide—until they discover something that changes everything…

Available on Amazon

The Watson Chronicles

Not all the myths of monsters lurking in the dark are just stories. When Doctor Watson first took rooms with Sherlock Holmes at 221b Baker Street, he found himself embroiled in a world of crime and intrigue he could barely comprehend.

One year on, Watson's now confident about assisting the detective, no matter how macabre the case might be. So when a young coalman from the Yorkshire Moors appears at their door, begging for help to locate his beloved sister who disappeared two days before under mysterious circumstances, Holmes and Watson can barely contain their excitement. But that enthusiasm soon turns to horror when Holmes uncovers the enigma of the tiger's claws—and places them both in the sights of a murderous madman...

Available on Amazon

The Watson Chronicles

Christopher D. Abbott, Michael Jan Friedman, and Aaron Rosenberg team up to bring you a stunning collection of four new Sherlock Holmes adventures.

From the cobbled streets of smog-filled London to the sweet country air of Scotland and beyond, Sherlock Holmes and his faithful friend Dr. John Watson embark on cases that test the detective's intellectual prowess, as well as his affinity for the unusual and the bizarre. Pull up a chair and prepare yourself to hear these cases . . . by candlelight.

Available on Amazon

Printed in Great Britain
by Amazon